POEMS FOR TRAVELLERS

POEMS FOR TRAVELLERS

With an introduction by
PAUL THEROUX

Selection and arrangement by
GABY MORGAN

MACMILLAN COLLECTOR'S LIBRARY

This collection first published 2019 by Macmillan Collector's Library

This edition first published 2024 by Macmillan Collector's Library
an imprint of Pan Macmillan
The Smithson, 6 Briset Street, London ECIM 5NR
EU representative: Macmillan Publishers Ireland Ltd, 1st Floor,
The Liffey Trust Centre, 117-126 Sheriff Street Upper,
Dublin 1, DOI YC43
Associated companies throughout the world
www.panmacmillan.com

ISBN 978-1-0350-2677-7

Selection and arrangement © Macmillan Publishers International Ltd 2019
Introduction © Paul Theroux 2019

'Ithaka' on page 40 is from *C. P. Cavafy: Collected Poems*, Revised Edition
translated by Edmund Keeley and Philip Sherrard, ed. by George Savidis.
Translation copyright © 1975, 1992 by Edmund Keeley and Philip Sherrard.
Reprinted by permission of Princeton University Press.

1 3 5 7 9 8 6 4 2

A CIP catalogue record for this book is available from the British Library.

Cover and endpaper design: Daisy Bates, Pan Macmillan Art Department
Typeset in Plantin MT Std by Jouve (UK), Milton Keynes
Printed and bound in China by Imago

MIX
Paper | Supporting
responsible forestry
FSC
www.fsc.org
FSC® C116313

Visit **www.panmacmillan.com** to read more about all our books
and to buy them. You will also find features, author interviews and
news of any author events, and you can sign up for e-newsletters
so that you're always first to hear about our new releases.

For Sue and Peter Morgan – the most intrepid of travellers, weavers of great stories and photographers of cats, dogs and local wildlife the world over

Contents

viii

THE WAY THROUGH THE WOODS

WHERE GO THE BOATS?

BEAUTIFUL CITY

HOME, SWEET HOME

Introduction

PAUL THEROUX

The poem in its allusiveness and usual brevity is well suited to describing the disjunction, the alienation, the surrealism, the impressionism, the imagism, the shock and the dreamlike qualities of the travel experience. And so this is a collection to value. Its curious aspect is that while some of these poems are written by travellers, others are by poets who seldom went anywhere, and a number of them by poets who did not visit the places they extolled in their poems.

A telling detail often proves that the poet was an eyewitness. Here are exuberant selections by Lord Byron – excerpts from *Childe Harold's Pilgrimage* and other shorter, free-standing poems. The extract from *Don Juan* contains one of my favourite travel observations. Don Juan is at the Bosphorus, the wind blowing from the Black Sea, known in Byron's time – and earlier – as the Euxine Sea. As the waves 'lash and lave Europe and Asia', Byron writes:

> There's not a sea the passenger e'er pukes in,
> Turns up more dangerous breakers than the Euxine.

Yet experience isn't everything. In spite of Rudyard Kipling's evocation of the Burmese city of Mandalay in his magnificent poem of the same name, the poet never visited the city – he saw a bit of Rangoon in a brief one-day touristic shore excursion when his ship stopped there. Nor did Edgar Allan Poe ever see the fabled city of Eldorado:

> 'Over the Mountains
>   Of the Moon,
> Down the Valley of the Shadow,
>   Ride, boldly ride,'
>   The shade replied,
> 'If you seek for Eldorado!'

Well, no one ever saw Eldorado, though many sought it. Poe was not much of a traveller; he visited England briefly but spent most of his life shuttling from New York to Baltimore, yet he was a brilliant imaginer of distant lands.

On his one trip out of the United States, Walt Whitman travelled to Canada in the summer of 1880, and he sailed down the Mississippi River as he describes in 'On Journeys Through the States' ('We pass through Kanada, the North-east, the vast valley of the Mississippi . . .'). But he lived most of his life in Brooklyn, New York, which is why his 'Crossing Brooklyn Ferry' – a trip he must have taken many times – is so achieved:

> And you that shall cross from shore to shore years
>   hence are more to me, and more in my
>   meditations, than you might suppose.

And the same note of urban experience can be found in the work of Sara Teasdale – a New Yorker – especially in her poem 'Broadway':

> This is the quiet hour; the theaters
>   Have gathered in their crowds, and steadily
>   The million lights blaze on for few to see,

Robbing the sky of stars that should be hers.
A woman waits with bag and shabby furs . . .

Similarly, the freshness of familiarity in her 'Union Square':

> With the man I love who loves me not,
>   I walked in the street-lamps' flare;
> We watched the world go home that night
>   In a flood through Union Square.

The authenticity and acute sadness in Claude McKay's 'The Tropics in New York' are vivid:

> Bananas ripe and green, and ginger-root,
>   Cocoa in pods and alligator pears,
> And tangerines and mangoes and grape fruit,
>   Fit for the highest prize at parish fairs . . .

And ends:

> My eyes grew dim, and I could no more gaze;
>   A wave of longing through my body swept,
> And, hungry for the old, familiar ways,
>   I turned aside and bowed my head and wept.

McKay's nostalgia for Jamaica, where he was born in 1889, is palpable, yet he did not return to the island. After emigrating to New York City he travelled widely, to Europe, to North Africa, and in the 1920s to the Soviet Union to attend the Communist Party's Fourth Congress.

McKay's peregrinations are in great contrast to Emily Dickinson's non-travelling. She is represented here by three stark poems. 'To shut our eyes is Travel,' Dickinson wrote to a friend in 1870. By then, aged forty, she had been housebound for almost ten years, and she had another fifteen reclusive years to live. She had begun her studies at Mount Holyoke College in South Hadley, about ten miles from her home in Amherst, Massachusetts, but she only lasted a year and, homesick, returned to the family home. 'Home is a holy thing – nothing of doubt or distrust can enter its blessed portals,' she wrote in a letter to her brother. And 'Duty is black and brown – home is bright and shining.' And again, home 'is brighter than all the world beside'.

I think we can be certain that John Masefield never sat in a 150-foot-long, pre-Christian war galley known as a quinquireme (five rowers per side), but his poem 'Cargoes' is nonetheless stirring ('Quinquireme of Nineveh from distant Ophir . . .'). Robert Louis Stevenson was prescient in his classic 'Travel', from *A Child's Garden of Verses* ('I should like to rise and go/Where the golden apples grow'), because he actually got himself from Edinburgh to Samoa in the South Pacific, and lived there until his death.

We know that Wordsworth stood on Westminster Bridge and wrote:

> Earth has not anything to show more fair:
> Dull would he be of soul who could pass by
> A sight so touching in its majesty . . .

And the natural world of the Lake District in Wordsworth's other poems was observed at first hand too, because Wordsworth was a tremendous hiker. He walked around Ireland, Scotland and Wales. In his fifties, he made walking tours to the Continent, rambling up and down France, Holland, Switzerland, Italy and elsewhere, writing the whole time. Even in his sixties he was able to walk twenty miles a day. His sister Dorothy wrote, 'And as to the climbing of mountains, the hardiest and youngest are yet hardly a match for him.' At the age of seventy Wordsworth climbed Helvellyn, the third-highest peak in the Lake District at over 3,000 feet.

Although C. P. Cavafy was Greek, and spent his life in Alexandria, Egypt, it's possible that he visited the island of Ithaca in the Ionian Sea. But his poem 'Ithaka' is inspired not by a trip but by *The Odyssey*, and I should say that if this book contained nothing more than this poem with its startling first lines:

> When you set out for Ithaka
> ask that your way be long,
> full of adventure, full of instruction . . .

I would regard it as worth keeping, cherishing and memorizing as a source of inspiration. But there is much more here, including poets I'd never heard of, such as the American Rachel Field. Her simple-seeming poem 'If Once You Have Slept on an Island' begins:

> If once you have slept on an island
> You'll never be quite the same . . .

Looking into her biography I discover Rachel Field to have been both prolific and prize-winning, a novelist as well as a poet. According to the American critic Ruth Hill Viguers she was 'fifteen when she first visited the state of Maine and fell under the spell of its "island-scattered coast"'. It so happens that like Rachel Field I have slept on an island off the Maine coast, as she did, and felt transformed.

Another discovery: most people think that the celebrated American poet Maya Angelou wrote the lines 'I know why the caged bird sings' – the title of one of her books. But readers of this volume will learn that these words were the work of Paul Laurence Dunbar in 'Sympathy':

> I know why the caged bird sings, ah me,
> When his wing is bruised and his bosom sore, –
> When he beats his bars and would be free;
> It is not a carol of joy or glee,
> But a prayer that he sends from his deep heart's core,
> But a plea, that upward to Heaven he flings –
> I know why the caged bird sings!

It is a personal satisfaction that this collection includes some of my favourite poems, and poems I have quoted in my own travel books. I love Shelley's 'Ozymandias' for illustrating the vanity of human wishes, with its arresting first lines:

> I met a traveller from an antique land
> Who said: Two vast and trunkless legs of stone
> Stand in the desert.

And Tennyson's 'Ulysses' is another favourite:

> Come, my friends,
> 'Tis not too late to seek a newer world.
> Push off, and sitting well in order smite
> The sounding furrows; for my purpose holds
> To sail beyond the sunset, and the baths
> Of all the western stars, until I die.
> It may be that the gulfs will wash us down:
> It may be we shall touch the Happy Isles . . .

Indeed, this poem gave me a title for one of my travel books.

'Ulysses' is heroic. Thomas Hardy's 'Departure Platform' is small-scale, a parting, intensely personal and moving, a poem to savour:

> We kissed at the barrier; and passing through
> She left me . . .

The same plain, melancholy note is struck in Edna St Vincent Millay's 'The Unexplorer':

> There was a road ran past our house
> Too lovely to explore.
> I asked my mother once – she said
> That if you followed where it led
> It brought you to the milk-man's door.
> (That's why I have not traveled more.)

Here is a collection of travel poetry composed by real travellers, weekending tourists, feverish fantasists, bluffers, dreamers, brave adventurers and resolute stay-at-homes. It succeeds in what poetry does best – inspires and consoles, reminds us of who we are, where we've been, and where we might want to go next.

POEMS FOR TRAVELLERS

THERE ARE NO FOREIGN LANDS

from The Silverado Squatters

There are no foreign lands. It is the traveller only who is foreign.

Robert Louis Stevenson (1850–1894)

A Prayer for Travellers

May the road rise up to meet you.
May the wind be always at your back.
May the sun shine warm upon your face;
The rains fall soft upon your fields.
And until we meet again,
May God hold you in the palm of His hand.

Anon.

On the World

The world's an inn; and I her guest.
I eat; I drink; I take my rest.
My hostess, nature, does deny me
Nothing, wherewith she can supply me;
Where, having stayed a while, I pay
Her lavish bills, and go my way.

Francis Quarles (1592–1644)

from Childe Harold's Pilgrimage

There is a pleasure in the pathless woods,
There is a rapture on the lonely shore,
There is society where none intrudes,
By the deep Sea, and music in its roar:
I love not Man the less, but Nature more,
From these our interviews, in which I steal
From all I may be, or have been before,
To mingle with the Universe, and feel
What I can ne'er express, yet cannot all conceal.

Roll on, thou deep and dark blue Ocean – roll!
Ten thousand fleets sweep over thee in vain;
Man marks the earth with ruin – his control
Stops with the shore; – upon the watery plain
The wrecks are all thy deed, nor doth remain
A shadow of man's ravage, save his own,
When, for a moment, like a drop of rain,
He sinks into thy depths with bubbling groan,
Without a grave, unknell'd, uncoffin'd, and unknown.

His steps are not upon thy paths, – thy fields
Are not a spoil for him, – thou dost arise
And shake him from thee; the vile strength he wields
For earth's destruction thou dost all despise,
Spurning him from thy bosom to the skies,
And send'st him, shivering in thy playful spray
And howling, to his Gods, where haply lies
His petty hope in some near port or bay,
And dashest him again to earth: – there let him lay.

George Gordon, Lord Byron (1788–1824)

On First Looking into Chapman's Homer

Much have I travell'd in the realms of gold,
  And many goodly states and kingdoms seen;
  Round many western islands have I been
Which bards in fealty to Apollo hold.
Oft of one wide expanse had I been told
  That deep-brow'd Homer ruled as his demesne;
  Yet did I never breathe its pure serene
Till I heard Chapman speak out loud and bold:
Then felt I like some watcher of the skies
  When a new planet swims into his ken;
Or like stout Cortez when with eagle eyes
  He star'd at the Pacific – and all his men
Look'd at each other with a wild surmise –
  Silent, upon a peak in Darien.

John Keats (1795–1821)

Heaven-Haven

I have desired to go
    Where springs not fail,
To fields where flies no sharp and sided hail
And a few lilies blow.

And I have asked to be
    Where no storms come,
Where the green swell is in the havens dumb,
And out of the swing of the sea.

Gerard Manley Hopkins (1844–1889)

Travel

I should like to rise and go
Where the golden apples grow;
Where below another sky
Parrot islands anchored lie,
And, watched by cockatoos and goats,
Lonely Crusoes building boats;
Where in sunshine reaching out
Eastern cities, miles about,
Are with mosque and minaret
Among sandy gardens set,
And the rich goods from near and far
Hang for sale in the bazaar;
Where the Great Wall round China goes,
And on one side the desert blows,
And with bell and voice and drum,
Cities on the other hum;
Where are forests, hot as fire,
Wide as England, tall as a spire,
Full of apes and coco-nuts
And the negro hunters' huts;
Where the knotty crocodile
Lies and blinks in the Nile,
And the red flamingo flies
Hunting fish before his eyes;
Where in jungles, near and far,
Man-devouring tigers are,
Lying close and giving ear
Lest the hunt be drawing near,
Or a comer-by be seen
Swinging in a palanquin;
Where among the desert sands

Some deserted city stands,
All its children, sweep and prince,
Grown to manhood ages since,
Not a foot in street or house,
Not a stir of child or mouse,
And when kindly falls the night,
In all the town no spark of light.
There I'll come when I'm a man
With a camel caravan;
Light a fire in the gloom
Of some dusty dining-room;
See the pictures on the walls,
Heroes, fights and festivals;
And in a corner find the toys
Of the old Egyptian boys.

Robert Louis Stevenson (1850–1894)

from My Lost Youth

Often I think of the beautiful town
   That is sealed by the sea;
Often in thought go up and down
The pleasant streets of that dear old town,
   And my youth comes back to me.
      And a verse of a Lapland song
      Is haunting my memory still:
      'A boy's will is the wind's will,
And the thoughts of youth are long, long thoughts.'

. . .

Strange to me now are the forms I meet
   When I visit the dear old town;
But the native air is pure and sweet,
And the trees that o'ershadow each well-known street,
   As they balance up and down,
      Are singing the beautiful song,
      Are sighing and whispering still:
      'A boy's will is the wind's will,
And the thoughts of youth are long, long thoughts.'

And Deering's Woods are fresh and fair,
   And with joy that is almost pain
My heart goes back to wander there,
And among the dreams of the days that were,
   I find my lost youth again.
      And the strange and beautiful song,

The groves are repeating it still:
  'A boy's will is the wind's will,
And the thoughts of youth are long, long thoughts.'

Henry Wadsworth Longfellow (1807–1882)

Windy Nights

Whenever the moon and the stars are set,
   Whenever the wind is high,
All night long in the dark and wet,
   A man goes riding by.
Late in the night when the fires are out,
Why does he gallop and gallop about?

Whenever the trees are crying aloud,
   And ships are tossed at sea,
By, on the highway, low and loud,
   By at the gallop goes he.
By at the gallop he goes, and then
By he comes back at the gallop again.

Robert Louis Stevenson (1850–1894)

The Vagabond

Give to me the life I love,
  Let the lave go by me,
Give the jolly heaven above
  And the byway nigh me.
Bed in the bush with stars to see,
  Bread I dip in the river—
There's the life for a man like me,
  There's the life forever.

Let the blow fall soon or late,
  Let what will be o'er me;
Give the face of earth around
  And the road before me.
Wealth I seek not, hope nor love,
  Nor a friend to know me;
All I seek, the heaven above
  And the road below me.

Or let autumn fall on me
  Where afield I linger,
Silencing the bird on tree,
  Biting the blue finger,
White as meal the frosty field –
  Warm the fireside haven –
Not to autumn will I yield,
  Nor to winter even!

Let the blow fall soon or late,
  Let what will be o'er me;
Give the face of earth around,
  And the road before me.

Wealth I ask not, hope nor love,
　Nor a friend to know me;
All I ask the heaven above,
　And the road below me.

Robert Louis Stevenson (1850–1894)

On Journeys Through the States

On journeys through the States we start,
(Ay through the world, urged by these songs,
Sailing henceforth to every land, to every sea,)
We willing learners of all, teachers of all, and
    lovers of all.

We have watch'd the seasons dispensing themselves
    and passing one,
And have said, Why should not a man or woman do
    as much as the seasons, and effuse as much?

We dwell a while in every city and town,
We pass through Kanada, the North-east, the vast
    valley of the Mississippi, and the Southern States,
We confer on equal terms with each of the States,
We make trial of ourselves and invite men and women
    to hear,
We say to ourselves, Remember, fear not, be candid,
    promulge the body and the soul,
Dwell a while and pass on, be copious, temperate,
    chaste, magnetic,
And what you effuse may then return as the seasons
    return,
And may be just as much as the seasons.

Walt Whitman (1819–1892)

Songs of Travel, X

I know not how it is with you –
    I love the first and last,
The whole field of the present view,
    The whole flow of the past.

One tittle of the things that are,
    Nor you should change nor I –
One pebble in our path – one star
    In all our heaven of sky.

Our lives, and every day and hour,
    One symphony appear:
One road, one garden – every flower
    And every bramble dear.

Robert Louis Stevenson (1850–1894)

from A Song About Myself

I

There was a naughty boy,
  A naughty boy was he,
He would not stop at home,
  He could not quiet be –
    He took
    In his knapsack
    A book
    Full of vowels
    And a shirt
    With some towels,
    A slight cap
    For night cap,
    A hair brush,
    Comb ditto,
    New stockings
    For old ones
    Would split O!
    This knapsack
    Tight at's back
    He rivetted close
And followed his nose
  To the north,
  To the north,
And follow'd his nose
  To the north.

II

There was a naughty boy
  And a naughty boy was he,
For nothing would he do
  But scribble poetry –
      He took
      An ink stand
      In his hand
      And a pen
      Big as ten
      In the other,
      And away
      In a pother
      He ran
      To the mountains
      And fountains
      And ghostes
      And postes
      And witches
      And ditches
      And wrote
      In his coat
      When the weather
      Was cool,
      Fear of gout,
      And without
      When the weather
      Was warm –
      Och the charm
      When we choose
To follow one's nose
      To the north,

To the north,
To follow one's nose
To the north!

IV

There was a naughty boy,
  And a naughty boy was he,
He ran away to Scotland
  The people for to see –
    There he found
    That the ground
    Was as hard,
    That a yard
    Was as long,
    That a song
    Was as merry,
    That a cherry
    Was as red,
    That lead
    Was as weighty,
    That fourscore
    Was as eighty,
    That a door
    Was as wooden
    As in England –
So he stood in his shoes
  And he wonder'd,
  He wonder'd,
He stood in his
  Shoes and he wonder'd.

John Keats (1795–1821)

18

The Tables Turned

Up! up! my Friend, and quit your books;
Or surely you'll grow double:
Up! up! my Friend, and clear your looks;
Why all this toil and trouble?

The sun, above the mountain's head,
A freshening lustre mellow
Through all the long green fields has spread,
His first sweet evening yellow.

Books! 'tis a dull and endless strife:
Come, hear the woodland linnet,
How sweet his music! on my life,
There's more of wisdom in it.

And hark! how blithe the throstle sings!
He, too, is no mean preacher:
Come forth into the light of things,
Let Nature be your Teacher.

William Wordsworth (1770–1850)

from Song of the Open Road

Afoot and light-hearted I take to the open road,
Healthy, free, the world before me,
The long brown path before me leading me wherever
    I choose.

Henceforth I ask not good-fortune, I myself am
    good-fortune.
Henceforth I whimper no more, postpone no more,
    need nothing,
Done with indoor complaints, libraries, querulous
    criticisms,
Strong and content I travel the open road.

Walt Whitman (1819–1892)

The Journey

The morning sea of silence broke into ripples of bird
    songs;
and the flowers were all merry by the roadside;
and the wealth of gold was scattered through the rift
    of the clouds
while we busily went on our way and paid no heed.

We sang no glad songs nor played;
we went not to the village for barter;
we spoke not a word nor smiled;
we lingered not on the way.
We quickened our pace more and more as the time
    sped by.

The sun rose to the mid sky and doves cooed in the
    shade.
Withered leaves danced and whirled in the hot air of
    noon.
The shepherd boy drowsed and dreamed in the
    shadow of the banyan tree,
and I laid myself down by the water
and stretched my tired limbs on the grass.

My companions laughed at me in scorn;
they held their heads high and hurried on;
they never looked back nor rested;
they vanished in the distant blue haze.

They crossed many meadows and hills,
and passed through strange, far-away countries.

All honour to you, heroic host of the interminable
      path!
Mockery and reproach pricked me to rise,
but found no response in me.

I gave myself up for lost
in the depth of a glad humiliation
– in the shadow of a dim delight.

The repose of the sun-embroidered green gloom
slowly spread over my heart.
I forgot for what I had travelled,
and I surrendered my mind without struggle
to the maze of shadows and songs.

At last, when I woke from my slumber and opened
      my eyes,
I saw thee standing by me, flooding my sleep with thy
      smile.
How I had feared that the path was long and
      wearisome,
and the struggle to reach thee was hard!

Rabindranath Tagore (1861–1941)

Sonnet – to an American
Painter Departing for Europe

Thine eyes shall see the light of distant skies:
  Yet, Cole! thy heart shall bear to Europe's strand
  A living image of thy native land,
Such as on thy own glorious canvass lies
Lone lakes – savannahs where the bison roves –
  Rocks rich with summer garlands – solemn streams –
  Skies, where the desert eagle wheels and screams –
Spring bloom and autumn blaze of boundless groves.
Fair scenes shall greet thee where thou goest – fair,
  But different – every where the trace of men,
  Paths, homes, graves, ruins, from the lowest glen
To where life shrinks from the fierce Alpine air.
  Gaze on them, till the tears shall dim thy sight,
  But keep that earlier, wilder image bright.

William Cullen Bryant (1794–1878)

Out Where the West Begins

Out where the handclasp's a little stronger,
Out where the smile dwells a little longer,
　That's where the West begins;
Out where the sun is a little brighter,
Where the snows that fall are a trifle whiter,
Where the bonds of home are a wee bit tighter, –
　That's where the West begins.

Out where the skies are a trifle bluer,
Out where friendship's a little truer,
　That's where the West begins;
Out where a fresher breeze is blowing,
Where there's laughter in every streamlet flowing,
Where there's more of reaping and less of sowing, –
　That's where the West begins.

Out where the world is in the making,
Where fewer hearts in despair are aching,
　That's where the West begins;
Where there's more of singing and less of sighing,
Where there's more of giving and less of buying,
And a man makes friends without half trying –
　That's where the West begins.

Arthur Chapman (1873–1935)

A Lover's Journey

When a lover hies abroad
Looking for his love,
Azrael smiling sheathes his sword,
Heaven smiles above.
Earth and sea
His servants be,
And to lesser compass round,
That his love be sooner found!

Rudyard Kipling (1865–1936)

Historical Associations

Dear Uncle Jim, this garden ground
That now you smoke your pipe around,
Has seen immortal actions done
And valiant battles lost and won.

Here we had best on tip-toe tread,
While I for safety march ahead,
For this is that enchanted ground
Where all who loiter slumber sound.

Here is the sea, here is the sand,
Here is simple Shepherd's Land,
Here are the fairy hollyhocks,
And there are Ali Baba's rocks.

But yonder, see! apart and high,
Frozen Siberia lies; where I,
With Robert Bruce and William Tell,
Was bound by an enchanter's spell.

There, then, awhile in chains we lay,
In wintry dungeons, far from day;
But ris'n at length, with might and main,
Our iron fetters burst in twain.

Then all the horns were blown in town;
And to the ramparts clanging down,
All the giants leaped to horse
And charged behind us through the gorse.

On we rode, the others and I,
Over the mountains blue, and by
The Silver River, the sounding sea
And the robber woods of Tartary.

A thousand miles we galloped fast,
And down the witches' lane we passed,
And rode amain, with brandished sword,
Up to the middle, through the ford.

Last we drew rein – a weary three –
Upon the lawn, in time for tea,
And from our steeds alighted down
Before the gates of Babylon.

Robert Louis Stevenson (1850–1894)

from *Twelfth Night*

O Mistress mine, where are you roaming?
O stay and hear! your true-love's coming
That can sing both high and low;
Trip no further, pretty sweeting,
Journeys end in lovers' meeting –
Every wise man's son doth know.

What is love? 'tis not hereafter;
Present mirth hath present laughter;
What's to come is still unsure:
In delay there lies no plenty, –
Then come kiss me, Sweet-and-twenty,
Youth's a stuff will not endure.

William Shakespeare (1564–1616)

Freedom

Give me the long, straight road before me,
  A clear, cold day with a nipping air,
Tall, bare trees to run on beside me,
  A heart that is light and free from care.
Then let me go! – I care not whither
  My feet may lead, for my spirit shall be
Free as the brook that flows to the river,
  Free as the river that flows to the sea.

Olive Runner

IN XANADU

Kubla Khan

In Xanadu did Kubla Khan
A stately pleasure-dome decree:
Where Alph, the sacred river, ran
Through caverns measureless to man
Down to a sunless sea.
So twice five miles of fertile ground
With walls and towers were girdled round:
And there were gardens bright with sinuous rills,
Where blossomed many an incense-bearing tree;
And here were forests ancient as the hills,
Enfolding sunny spots of greenery.
But oh! that deep romantic chasm which slanted
Down the green hill athwart a cedarn cover!
A savage place! as holy and enchanted
As e'er beneath a waning moon was haunted
By woman wailing for her demon-lover!
And from this chasm, with ceaseless turmoil
    seething,
As if this earth in fast thick pants were breathing,
A mighty fountain momently was forced:
Amid whose swift half-intermitted burst
Huge fragments vaulted like rebounding hail,
Or chaffy grain beneath the thresher's flail:
And 'mid these dancing rocks at once and ever
It flung up momently the sacred river.
Five miles meandering with a mazy motion
Through wood and dale the sacred river ran,
Then reached the caverns measureless to man,
And sank in tumult to a lifeless ocean:
And 'mid this tumult Kubla heard from far
Ancestral voices prophesying war!

The shadow of the dome of pleasure
Floated midway on the waves;
Where was heard the mingled measure
From the fountain and the caves.
It was a miracle of rare device,
A sunny pleasure-dome with caves of ice!
A damsel with a dulcimer
In a vision once I saw:
It was an Abyssinian maid,
And on her dulcimer she played,
Singing of Mount Abora.

Could I revive within me
Her symphony and song,
To such a deep delight 'twould win me,
That with music loud and long,
I would build that dome in air,
That sunny dome! those caves of ice!
And all who heard should see them there,
And all should cry, Beware! Beware!
His flashing eyes, his floating hair!
Weave a circle round him thrice,
And close your eyes with holy dread,
For he on honey-dew hath fed,
And drunk the milk of Paradise.

Samuel Taylor Coleridge (1772–1834)

from *A Midsummer Night's Dream*

More strange than true! I never may believe
These antique fables, nor these fairy toys.
Lovers and madmen have such seething brains,
Such shaping fantasies, that apprehend
More than cool reason ever comprehends.
The lunatic, the lover and the poet
Are of imagination all compact.
One sees more devils than vast hell can hold:
That is the madman. The lover, all as frantic,
Sees Helen's beauty in a brow of Egypt.
The poet's eye, in fine frenzy rolling,
Doth glance from heaven to earth, from earth to heaven,
And as imagination bodies forth
The forms of things unknown, the poet's pen
Turns them to shapes, and gives to airy nothing
A local habitation and a name.
Such tricks hath strong imagination,
That if it would but apprehend some joy,
It comprehends some bringer of that joy;
Or in the night, imagining some fear,
How easy is a bush suppos'd a bear!

William Shakespeare (1564–1616)

from Shah-Jahan

You knew, Emperor of India, Shah-Jahan,
   That life, youth, wealth, renown
All float away down the stream of time.
     Your only dream
Was to preserve forever your heart's pain.
   The harsh thunder of imperial power
     Would fade into sleep
   Like a sunset's crimson splendour,
     But it was your hope
That at least a single, eternally-heaved sigh would stay
     To grieve the sky.
   Though emeralds, rubies, pearls are all
But as the glitter of a rainbow tricking out empty air
     And must pass away,
   Yet still one solitary tear
   Would hang on the cheek of time
     In the form
   Of this white and gleaming Taj Mahal.

     O human heart,
    You have no time
  To look back at anyone again,
      No time.
You are driven by life's quick spate
  On and on from landing to landing,
    Loading cargo here,
      Unloading there.

In your garden, the south wind's murmurs
    May enchant spring *madhabi*-creepers
Into suddenly filling your quivering lap with flowers –
    Their petals are scattered in the dust come twilight.
        You have no time –
        You raise from the dew of another night
    New blossom in your groves, new jasmine
To dress with tearful gladness the votive tray
        Of a later season.
            O human heart,
        All that you gather is thrown
To the edge of the path by the end of each night
    and day.
    You have no time to look back again,
        No time, no time . . .

Rabindranath Tagore (1861–1941)

Eldorado

Gaily bedight,
   A gallant knight,
In sunshine and in shadow,
   Had journeyed long,
   Singing a song,
In search of Eldorado.

But he grew old –
   This knight so bold –
And o'er his heart a shadow
   Fell, as he found
   No spot of ground
That looked like Eldorado.

And, as his strength
   Failed him at length,
He met a pilgrim shadow –
   'Shadow,' said he,
   'Where can it be –
This land of Eldorado?'

'Over the Mountains
   Of the Moon,
Down the Valley of the Shadow,
   Ride, boldly ride,'
   The shade replied,
'If you seek for Eldorado!'

Edgar Allan Poe (1809–1849)

Ozymandias

I met a traveller from an antique land
Who said: Two vast and trunkless legs of stone
Stand in the desert. Near them, on the sand,
Half sunk, a shattered visage lies, whose frown,
And wrinkled lip, and sneer of cold command
Tell that its sculptor well those passions read
Which yet survive (stamped on these lifeless things)
The hand that mocked them and the heart that fed:
And on the pedestal these words appear:
'My name is Ozymandias, King of Kings:
Look on my works, ye Mighty, and despair!'
Nothing beside remains. Round the decay
Of that colossal wreck, boundless and bare
The lone and level sands stretch far away.

Percy Bysshe Shelley (1792–1822)

Ithaka

When you set out for Ithaka
ask that your way be long,
full of adventure, full of instruction.
The Laistrygonians and the Cyclops,
angry Poseidon – do not fear them:
such as these you will never find
as long as your thought is lofty, as long as a rare
emotion touch your spirit and your body.
The Laistrygonians and the Cyclops,
wild Poseidon – you will not meet them
unless you carry them in your soul,
unless your soul raises them up before you.

Ask that your way be long.
At many a summer dawn to enter
– with what gratitude, what joy –
ports seen for the first time;
to stop at Phoenician trading centres
and to buy good merchandise,
mother of pearl and coral, amber and ebony,
sensuous perfumes of every kind,
sensuous perfumes as lavishly as you can;
to visit many Egyptian cities,
to gather stores of knowledge from the learned.

Have Ithaka always in your mind.
Your arrival there is what you are destined for.
But do not in the least hurry the journey.
Better that it lasts for years,
so that when you reach the island you are old,

rich with all you have gained on the way,
not expecting Ithaka to give you wealth.

Ithaka gave you the splendid journey.
Without her you would not have set out.
She hasn't anything else to give you.
And if you find her poor, Ithaka has not deceived you.
So wise have you become, of such experience,
that already you will have understood what these
   Ithakas mean.

                           C. P. Cavafy (1863–1933)

Ulysses

It little profits that an idle king,
By this still hearth, among these barren crags,
Match'd with an aged wife, I mete and dole
Unequal laws unto a savage race,
That hoard, and sleep, and feed, and know not me.
I cannot rest from travel: I will drink
Life to the lees: All times I have enjoy'd
Greatly, have suffer'd greatly, both with those
That loved me, and alone, on shore, and when
Thro' scudding drifts the rainy Hyades
Vext the dim sea: I am become a name;
For always roaming with a hungry heart
Much have I seen and known; cities of men
And manners, climates, councils, governments,
Myself not least, but honour'd of them all;
And drunk delight of battle with my peers,
Far on the ringing plains of windy Troy.
I am a part of all that I have met;
Yet all experience is an arch wherethro'
Gleams that untravell'd world whose margin fades
For ever and for ever when I move.
How dull it is to pause, to make an end,
To rust unburnish'd, not to shine in use!
As tho' to breathe were life. Life piled on life
Were all too little, and of one to me
Little remains: but every hour is saved
From that eternal silence, something more,
A bringer of new things; and vile it were
For some three suns to store and hoard myself,
And this gray spirit yearning in desire
To follow knowledge like a sinking star,

Beyond the utmost bound of human thought.

    This is my son, mine own Telemachus,
To whom I leave the sceptre and the isle, –
Well-loved of me, discerning to fulfil
This labour, by slow prudence to make mild
A rugged people, and thro' soft degrees
Subdue them to the useful and the good.
Most blameless is he, centred in the sphere
Of common duties, decent not to fail
In offices of tenderness, and pay
Meet adoration to my household gods,
When I am gone. He works his work, I mine.

    There lies the port; the vessel puffs her sail:
There gloom the dark, broad seas. My mariners,
Souls that have toil'd, and wrought, and thought with
   me –
That ever with a frolic welcome took
The thunder and the sunshine, and opposed
Free hearts, free foreheads – you and I are old;
Old age hath yet his honour and his toil;
Death closes all: but something ere the end,
Some work of noble note, may yet be done,
Not unbecoming men that strove with Gods.
The lights begin to twinkle from the rocks:
The long day wanes: the slow moon climbs: the deep
Moans round with many voices. Come, my friends,
'Tis not too late to seek a newer world.
Push off, and sitting well in order smite
The sounding furrows; for my purpose holds
To sail beyond the sunset, and the baths
Of all the western stars, until I die.
It may be that the gulfs will wash us down:
It may be we shall touch the Happy Isles,
And see the great Achilles, whom we knew.

Tho' much is taken, much abides; and tho'
We are not now that strength which in old days
Moved earth and heaven, that which we are, we are;
One equal temper of heroic hearts,
Made weak by time and fate, but strong in will
To strive, to seek, to find, and not to yield.

Alfred, Lord Tennyson (1809–1892)

Dream Land

Where sunless rivers weep
Their waves into the deep,
She sleeps a charmed sleep:
   Awake her not.
Led by a single star,
She came from very far
To seek where shadows are
   Her pleasant lot.

She left the rosy morn,
She left the fields of corn,
For twilight cold and lorn
   And water springs.
Through sleep, as through a veil,
She sees the sky look pale,
And hears the nightingale
   That sadly sings.

Rest, rest, a perfect rest
Shed over brow and breast;
Her face is toward the west,
   The purple land.
She cannot see the grain
Ripening on hill and plain;
She cannot feel the rain
   Upon her hand.

Rest, rest, for evermore
Upon a mossy shore;
Rest, rest at the heart's core

Till time shall cease:
Sleep that no pain shall wake,
Night that no morn shall break
Till joy shall overtake
  Her perfect peace.

Christina Rossetti (1830–1894)

Winter Journey Over The Hartz Mountain

Like the vulture
Who on heavy morning clouds
With gentle wing reposing
Looks for his prey, –
Hover, my song!

For a God hath
Unto each prescribed
His destined path,
Which the happy one
Runs o'er swiftly
To his glad goal:
He whose heart cruel
Fate hath contracted,
Struggles but vainly
Against all the barriers
The brazen thread raises,
But which the harsh shears
Must one day sever.

Through gloomy thickets
Presseth the wild deer on,
And with the sparrows
Long have the wealthy
Settled themselves in the marsh.

Easy 'tis following the chariot
That by Fortune is driven,
Like the baggage that moves
Over well-mended highways
After the train of a prince.

But who stands there apart?
In the thicket, lost is his path;
Behind him the bushes
Are closing together,
The grass springs up again,
The desert engulphs him.

Ah, who'll heal his afflictions,
To whom balsam was poison,
Who, from love's fullness,
Drank in misanthropy only?
First despised, and now a despiser,
He, in secret, wasteth
All that he is worth,
In a selfishness vain.
If there be, on thy psaltery,
Father of Love, but one tone
That to his ear may be pleasing,
Oh, then, quicken his heart!
Clear his cloud-enveloped eyes
Over the thousand fountains
Close by the thirsty one
In the desert.

Thou who createst much joy,
For each a measure o'erflowing,
Bless the sons of the chase
When on the track of the prey,
With a wild thirsting for blood,
Youthful and joyous
Avenging late the injustice
Which the peasant resisted
Vainly for years with his staff.

But the lonely one veil
Within thy gold clouds!
Surround with winter-green,
Until the roses bloom again,
The humid locks,
Oh Love, of thy minstrel!

With thy glimmering torch
Lightest thou him
Through the fords when 'tis night,
Over bottomless places
On desert-like plains;
With the thousand colours of morning
Gladd'nest his bosom;
With the fierce-biting storm
Bearest him proudly on high;
Winter torrents rush from the cliffs, –
Blend with his psalms;
An altar of grateful delight
He finds in the much-dreaded mountain's
Snow-begirded summit,
Which foreboding nations
Crown'd with spirit-dances.

Thou stand'st with breast inscrutable,
Mysteriously disclosed,
High o'er the wondering world,
And look'st from clouds
Upon its realms and its majesty,
Which thou from the veins of thy brethren
Near thee dost water.

Johann Wolfgang von Goethe (1749–1832)

The Golden Journey To Samarkand

I

We who with songs beguile your pilgrimage
And swear that Beauty lives though lilies die,
We Poets of the proud old lineage
Who sing to find your hearts, we know not why, –

What shall we tell you? Tales, marvellous tales
Of ships and stars and isles where good men rest,
Where nevermore the rose of sunset pales,
And winds and shadows fall towards the West:

And there the world's first huge white-bearded kings
In dim glades sleeping, murmur in their sleep,
And closer round their breasts the ivy clings,
Cutting its pathway slow and red and deep.

II

And how beguile you? Death has no repose
Warmer and deeper than the Orient sand
Which hides the beauty and bright faith of those
Who make the Golden Journey to Samarkand.

And now they wait and whiten peaceably,
Those conquerors, those poets, those so fair:
They know time comes, not only you and I,
But the whole world shall whiten, here or there;

When those long caravans that cross the plain
With dauntless feet and sound of silver bells

Put forth no more for glory or for gain,
Take no more solace from the palm-girt wells.

When the great markets by the sea shut fast
All that calm Sunday that goes on and on:
When even lovers find their peace at last,
And Earth is but a star, that once had shone.

James Elroy Flecker (1884–1915)

from The Rime of the Ancient Mariner

I

It is an ancient Mariner,
And he stoppeth one of three.
'By thy long grey beard and glittering eye,
Now wherefore stopp'st thou me?

The Bridegroom's doors are opened wide,
And I am next of kin;
The guests are met, the feast is set:
May'st hear the merry din.'

He holds him with his skinny hand,
'There was a ship,' quoth he.
'Hold off! unhand me, grey-beard loon!'
Eftsoons his hand dropt he.

He holds him with his glittering eye –
The Wedding-Guest stood still,
And listens like a three years' child:
The Mariner hath his will.

The Wedding-Guest sat on a stone:
He cannot choose but hear;
And thus spake on that ancient man,
The bright-eyed Mariner.

'The ship was cheered, the harbour cleared,
Merrily did we drop

Below the kirk, below the hill,
Below the lighthouse top.

The Sun came up upon the left,
Out of the sea came he!
And he shone bright, and on the right
Went down into the sea.

Higher and higher every day,
Till over the mast at noon –'
The Wedding-Guest here beat his breast,
For he heard the loud bassoon.

The bride hath paced into the hall,
Red as a rose is she;
Nodding their heads before her goes
The merry minstrelsy.

The Wedding-Guest he beat his breast,
Yet he cannot choose but hear;
And thus spake on that ancient man,
The bright-eyed Mariner.

'And now the STORM-BLAST came, and he
Was tyrannous and strong:
He struck with his o'ertaking wings,
And chased us south along.

With sloping masts and dipping prow,
As who pursued with yell and blow
Still treads the shadow of his foe,
And forward bends his head,
The ship drove fast, loud roared the blast,
And southward aye we fled.

And now there came both mist and snow,
And it grew wondrous cold:
And ice, mast-high, came floating by,
As green as emerald.

And through the drifts the snowy clifts
Did send a dismal sheen:
Nor shapes of men nor beasts we ken –
The ice was all between.

The ice was here, the ice was there,
The ice was all around:
It cracked and growled, and roared and howled,
Like noises in a swound!

At length did cross an Albatross,
Thorough the fog it came;
As if it had been a Christian soul,
We hailed it in God's name.

It ate the food it ne'er had eat,
And round and round it flew.
The ice did split with a thunder-fit;
The helmsman steered us through!

And a good south wind sprung up behind;
The Albatross did follow,
And every day, for food or play,
Came to the mariner's hollo!

In mist or cloud, on mast or shroud,
It perched for vespers nine;
Whiles all the night, through fog-smoke white,
Glimmered the white Moon-shine.'

'God save thee, ancient Mariner!
From the fiends, that plague thee thus! –
Why look'st thou so?' – 'With my cross-bow
I shot the ALBATROSS.'

Samuel Taylor Coleridge (1772–1834)

from Lycidas

Thus sang the uncouth swain to th'oaks and rills,
While the still morn went out with sandals grey;
He touched the tender stops of various quills,
With eager thought warbling his Doric lay:
And now the sun had stretched out all the hills,
And now was dropped into the western bay.
At last he rose, and twitched his mantle blue:
Tomorrow to fresh woods, and pastures new.

John Milton (1608–1674)

Dream-Land

By a route obscure and lonely,
Haunted by ill angels only,
Where an Eridolon, named NIGHT,
On a black throne reigns upright,
   I have reached these lands but newly
      From an ultimate dim Thule –
From a wild weird clime that lieth, sublime,
      Out of SPACE – out of TIME.
Bottomless vales and boundless floods,
And chasms, and caves and Titan woods,
With forms that no man can discover
For the tears that drip all over;
Mountains toppling evermore
Into seas without a shore;
Seas that restlessly aspire,
Surging, unto skies of fire;
Lakes that endlessly outspread
Their lone waters – lone and dead, –
Their still waters – still and chilly
With the snows of the lolling lily.

By the lakes that thus outspread
Their lone waters, lone and dead, –
Their sad waters, sad and chilly
With the snows of the lolling lily, –
By the mountains – near the river
Murmuring lowly, murmuring ever, –
By the grey woods, – by the swamp
Where the toad and the newt encamp, –
By the dismal tarns and pools
   Where dwell the Ghouls, –

By each spot the most unholy –
In each nook most melancholy, –
There the traveller meets, aghast,
Sheeted Memories of the Past –
Shrouded forms that start and sigh
As they pass the wanderer by –
White-robed forms of friends long given,
In agony, to the Earth – and Heaven.

For the heart whose woes are legion
'Tis a peaceful, soothing region –
For the spirit that walks in shadow
'Tis – oh 'tis an Eldorado!
But the traveller, travelling through it,
May not – dare not openly view it;
Never its mysteries are exposed
To the weak human eye unclosed;
So wills its King, who hath forbid
The uplifting of the fringéd lid;
And thus the sad Soul that here passes
Beholds it but through darkened glasses.

By a route obscure and lonely,
Haunted by ill angels only,
Where an Eridolon, named NIGHT,
On a black throne reigns upright,
I have wandered home but newly
From this ultimate dim Thule.

Edgar Allan Poe (1809–1849)

from *The Lady of Shalott*

I

On either side the river lie
Long fields of barley and of rye,
That clothe the wold and meet the sky;
And thro' the field the road runs by
   To many-tower'd Camelot;
And up and down the people go,
Gazing where the lilies blow
Round an island there below,
   The island of Shalott.

Willows whiten, aspens quiver,
Little breezes dusk and shiver
Thro' the wave that runs for ever
By the island in the river
   Flowing down to Camelot.
Four gray walls, and four gray towers,
Overlook a space of flowers,
And the silent isle imbowers
   The Lady of Shalott.

By the margin, willow-veil'd,
Slide the heavy barges trail'd
By slow horses; and unhail'd
The shallop flitteth silken-sail'd
   Skimming down to Camelot:
But who hath seen her wave her hand?
Or at the casement seen her stand?
Or is she known in all the land,
   The Lady of Shalott?

Only reapers, reaping early
In among the bearded barley,
Hear a song that echoes cheerly
From the river winding clearly,
   Down to tower'd Camelot:
And by the moon the reaper weary,
Piling sheaves in uplands airy,
Listening, whispers ''Tis the fairy
   Lady of Shalott.'

II

There she weaves by night and day
A magic web with colours gay.
She has heard a whisper say,
A curse is on her if she stay
   To look down to Camelot.
She knows not what the curse may be,
And so she weaveth steadily,
And little other care hath she,
   The Lady of Shalott.

And moving thro' a mirror clear
That hangs before her all the year,
Shadows of the world appear.
There she sees the highway near
   Winding down to Camelot:
There the river eddy whirls
And there the surly village-churls,
And the red cloaks of market girls
   Pass onward from Shalott.

Sometimes a troop of damsels glad,
An abbot on an ambling pad,

Sometimes a curly shepherd-lad,
Or long-hair'd page in crimson clad,
   Goes by to tower'd Camelot;
And sometimes thro' the mirror blue
The knights come riding two and two:
She hath no loyal knight and true,
   The Lady of Shalott.

But in her web she still delights
To weave the mirror's magic sights,
For often thro' the silent nights
A funeral, with plumes and lights,
   And music, went to Camelot:
Or when the moon was overhead,
Came two young lovers lately wed;
'I am half sick of shadows,' said
   The Lady of Shalott.

Alfred, Lord Tennyson (1809–1892)

from *The Tempest*: The Isle Is Full of Noises

Be not afeard. The isle is full of noises,
Sounds, and sweet airs that give delight and hurt not.
Sometimes a thousand twangling instruments
Will hum about mine ears, and sometime voices
That, if I then had waked after long sleep,
Will make me sleep again. And then, in dreaming,
The clouds methought would open and show riches
Ready to drop upon me, that when I waked
I cried to dream again.

William Shakespeare (1564–1616)

THE WAY THROUGH THE WOODS

The Way Through the Woods

They shut the road through the woods
  Seventy years ago.
Weather and rain have undone it again,
  And now you would never know
There was once a road through the woods
  Before they planted the trees.
It is underneath the coppice and heath,
  And the thin anemones.
Only the keeper sees
  That, where the ring-dove broods,
And the badgers roll at ease,
  There was once a road through the woods.

Yet, if you enter the woods
  Of a summer evening late,
When the night-air cools on the trout-ringed pools
  Where the otter whistles his mate,
(They fear not men in the woods,
  Because they see so few)
You will hear the beat of a horse's feet
  And the swish of a skirt in the dew,
  Steadily cantering through
The misty solitudes,
  As though they perfectly knew
The old lost road through the woods . . .
  But there is no road through the woods.

Rudyard Kipling (1865–1936)

Adlestrop

Yes, I remember Adlestrop –
The name, because one afternoon
Of heat the express-train drew up there
Unwontedly. It was late June.

The steam hissed. Someone cleared his throat.
No one left and no one came
On the bare platform. What I saw
Was Adlestrop – only the name

And willows, willow-herb, and grass,
And meadowsweet, and haycocks dry,
No whit less still and lonely fair
Than the high cloudlets in the sky.

And for that minute a blackbird sang
Close by, and round him, mistier,
Farther and farther, all the birds
Of Oxfordshire and Gloucestershire.

Edward Thomas (1878–1917)

My Heart's in the Highlands

My heart's in the Highlands, my heart is not here;
My heart's in the Highlands a-chasing the deer,
Chasing the wild deer and following the roe,
My heart's in the Highlands wherever I go.
Farewell to the Highlands, farewell to the North,
The birth-place of valour, the country of worth,
Wherever I wander, wherever I rove.
The hills of the highlands for ever I love.

Farewell to the mountains, high covered with snow;
Farewell to the straths and green valleys below:
Farewell to the forests and wild-hanging woods;
Farewell to the torrents and loud-pouring floods.
My heart's in the Highlands, my heart is not here;
My heart's in the Highlands a-chasing the deer;
Chasing the wild deer and following the roe,
My heart's in the Highlands, wherever I go.

Robert Burns (1759–1796)

Sing me a Song of a Lad that is Gone

Sing me a song of a lad that is gone,
Say, could that lad be I?
Merry of soul he sailed on a day
Over the sea to Skye.

Mull was astern, Rum on the port,
Eigg on the starboard bow;
Glory of youth glowed in his soul;
Where is that glory now?

Sing me a song of a lad that is gone,
Say, could that lad be I?
Merry of soul he sailed on a day
Over the sea to Skye.

Give me again all that was there,
Give me the sun that shone!
Give me the eyes, give me the soul,
Give me the lad that's gone!

Sing me a song of a lad that is gone,
Say, could that lad be I?
Merry of soul he sailed on a day
Over the sea to Skye.

Billow and breeze, islands and seas,
Mountains of rain and sun,
All that was good, all that was fair,
All that was me is gone.

Robert Louis Stevenson (1850–1894)

Loch Lomond

By yon bonnie banks and by yon bonnie braes,
Where the sun shines bright on Loch Lomond,
Where me and my true love were ever wont to gae
On the bonnie, bonnie banks o' Loch Lomond.

O ye'll tak' the high road, and I'll tak' the low road,
And I'll be in Scotland a'fore ye,
But me and my true love will never meet again,
On the bonnie, bonnie banks o' Loch Lomond.

'Twas there that we parted, in yon shady glen,
On the steep, steep side o' Ben Lomond,
Where in purple hue, the hieland hills we view,
And the moon coming out in the gloaming.

O ye'll tak' the high road, and I'll tak' the low road,
And I'll be in Scotland a'fore ye,
But me and my true love will never meet again,
On the bonnie, bonnie banks o' Loch Lomond.

The wee birdies sing and the wildflowers spring,
And in sunshine the waters are sleeping.
But the broken heart it kens nae second spring again,
Though the waeful may cease frae their grieving.

O ye'll tak' the high road, and I'll tak' the low road,
And I'll be in Scotland a'fore ye,
But me and my true love will never meet again,
On the bonnie, bonnie banks o' Loch Lomond.

Traditional

Highways and Byways

Highways for eident feet,
    That hae their mile to gae;
But byways when spring is sweet,
    And bloom is on the slae.

Highways till day is dune,
    The girr o' gear to ca';
But byways for star and mune,
    And wooers twa by twa.

Highways for wheel and whip,
    Till rigs are stibblet clear;
But byways for haw and hip,
    When robin's on the brier.

Aye it's on the highways
    The feck o' life maun gang;
But aye it's frae the byways
    Comes hame the happy sang.

Walter Wingate (1865–1918)

A Smuggler's Song

If you wake at midnight, and hear a horse's feet,
Don't go drawing back the blind, or looking in the
    street,
Them that ask no questions isn't told a lie.
Watch the wall, my darling, while the Gentlemen
    go by!
    Five and twenty ponies,
    Trotting through the dark –
    Brandy for the Parson,
    'Baccy for the Clerk;
    Laces for a lady; letters for a spy,
And watch the wall, my darling, while the Gentlemen
    go by!

Running round the woodlump if you chance to find
Little barrels, roped and tarred, all full of
    brandy-wine,
Don't you shout to come and look, nor use 'em for
    your play.
Put the brishwood back again – and they'll be gone
    next day!

If you see the stable-door setting open wide;
If you see a tired horse lying down inside;
If your mother mends a coat cut about and tore;
If the lining's wet and warm – don't you ask no more!

If you meet King George's men, dressed in blue and
    red,
You be careful what you say, and mindful what is said.

If they call you 'pretty maid', and chuck you 'neath
   the chin,
Don't you tell where no one is, nor yet where no one's
   been!

Knocks and footsteps round the house – whistles after
   dark –
You've no call for running out till the house-dogs
   bark.
Trusty's here, and *Pincher*'s here, and see how dumb
   they lie –
They don't fret to follow when the Gentlemen go by!

If you do as you've been told, likely there's chance,
You'll be give a dainty doll, all the way from France,
With a cap of Valenciennes, and a velvet hood –
A present from the Gentlemen, along o' being good!
      Five and twenty ponies,
      Trotting through the dark –
      Brandy for the Parson,
      'Baccy for the Clerk.
Them that asks no questions isn't told a lie –
Watch the wall, my darling, while the Gentlemen
   go by!

Rudyard Kipling (1865–1936)

The Lake Isle of Innisfree

I will arise and go now, and go to Innisfree,
And a small cabin build there, of clay and wattles
    made:
Nine bean-rows will I have there, a hive for the
    honey-bee,
And live alone in the bee-loud glade.

And I shall have some peace there, for peace comes
    dropping slow,
Dropping from the veils of the morning to where the
    cricket sings;
There midnight's all a glimmer, and noon a purple
    glow,
And evening full of the linnet's wings.

I will arise and go now, for always night and day
I hear lake water lapping with low sounds by the
    shore;
While I stand on the roadway, or on the pavements
    grey,
I hear it in the deep heart's core.

W. B. Yeats (1865–1939)

The Fiddler of Dooney

When I play my fiddle in Dooney,
Folk dance like a wave of the sea;
My cousin is a priest in Kilvarnet,
My brother in Mocharabuiee.

I passed my brother and cousin:
They read in their books of prayer;
I read in my book of songs
I bought at the Sligo fair.

When we come to the end of time
To Peter sitting in state,
He will smile on three old spirits,
But call me first through the gate;

For the good are always the merry,
Save for an evil chance,
And the merry love the fiddle,
And the merry love to dance:

And when the folk there spy me,
They will all come up to me,
With 'Here is the fiddler of Dooney!'
And dance like a wave of the sea.

W. B. Yeats (1865–1939)

The People of the Eastern Ice

The People of the Eastern Ice, they are melting like
    the snow –
They beg for coffee and sugar; they go where the
    white men go.
The People of the Western Ice, they learn to steal and
    fight;
They sell their furs to the trading-post; they sell their
    souls to the white.
The People of the Southern Ice, they trade with the
    whaler's crew;
Their women have many ribbons, but their tents are
    torn and few.
But the People of the Elder Ice, beyond the white
    man's ken –
Their spears are made of the narwhal-horn, and they
    are the last of the Men!

Rudyard Kipling (1865–1936)

from Elegy on Captain Cook

Ye, who ere-while for Cook's illustrious brow
Pluck'd the green laurel, and the oaken bough,
Hung the gay garlands on the trophied oars,
And pour'd his fame along a thousand shores,
Strike the slow death-bell! – weave the sacred verse,
And strew the cypress o'er his honour'd hearse;
In sad procession wander round the shrine,
And weep him mortal, whom ye sung divine!
  Say first, what Power inspir'd his dauntless breast
With scorn of danger, and inglorious rest,
To quit imperial London's gorgeous domes,
Where, deck'd in thousand tints, bright Pleasure
  roams;
In cups of summer-ice her nectar pours,
Or twines, 'mid wint'ry snows, her roseate bowers ...
Where Beauty moves with fascinating grace,
Calls the sweet blush to wanton o'er her face,
On each fond youth her soft artillery tries,
Aims her light smile, and rolls her frolic eyes:
What Power inspir'd his dauntless breast to brave
The scorch'd Equator, and th'Antarctic wave?

Anna Seward (1747–1809)

Home-Thoughts from Abroad

Oh, to be in England
Now that April's there,
And whoever wakes in England
Sees, some morning, unaware,
That the lowest boughs and the brushwood sheaf
Round the elm-tree bole are in tiny leaf,
While the chaffinch sings on the orchard bough
In England – now!

And after April, when May follows,
And the whitethroat builds, and all the swallows!
Hark, where my blossomed pear-tree in the hedge
Leans to the field and scatters on the clover
Blossoms and dewdrops – at the bent spray's edge –
That's the wise thrush; he sings each song twice over,
Lest you should think he never could recapture
The first fine careless rapture!
And though the fields look rough with hoary dew,
All will be gay when noontide wakes anew
The buttercups, the little children's dower
– Far brighter than this gaudy melon-flower!

Robert Browning (1812–1889)

This Lime-Tree Bower My Prison

Well, they are gone, and here must I remain,
This lime-tree bower my prison! I have lost
Beauties and feelings, such as would have been
Most sweet to my remembrance even when age
Had dimm'd mine eyes to blindness!
They, meanwhile,
Friends, whom I never more may meet again,
On springy heath, along the hill-top edge,
Wander in gladness, and wind down, perchance,
To that still roaring dell, of which I told;
The roaring dell, o'erwooded, narrow, deep,
And only speckled by the mid-day sun;
Where its slim trunk the ash from rock to rock
Flings arching like a bridge; – that branchless ash,
Unsunn'd and damp, whose few poor yellow leaves
Ne'er tremble in the gale, yet tremble still,
Fann'd by the water-fall! and there my friends
Behold the dark green file of long lank weeds,
That all at once (a most fantastic sight!)
Still nod and drip beneath the dripping edge
Of the blue clay-stone.

Now, my friends emerge
Beneath the wide wide Heaven – and view again
The many-steepled tract magnificent
Of hilly fields and meadows, and the sea,
With some fair bark, perhaps, whose sails light up
The slip of smooth clear blue betwixt two Isles
Of purple shadow! Yes! they wander on
In gladness all; but thou, methinks, most glad,
My gentle-hearted Charles! for thou hast pined

And hunger'd after Nature, many a year,
In the great City pent, winning thy way
With sad yet patient soul, through evil and pain
And strange calamity! Ah! slowly sink
Behind the western ridge, thou glorious Sun!
Shine in the slant beams of the sinking orb,
Ye purple heath-flowers! richlier burn, ye clouds!
Live in the yellow light, ye distant groves!
And kindle, thou blue Ocean! So my friend
Struck with deep joy may stand, as I have stood,
Silent with swimming sense; yea, gazing round
On the wide landscape, gaze till all doth seem
Less gross than bodily; and of such hues
As veil the Almighty Spirit, when yet he makes
Spirits perceive his presence.

A delight
Comes sudden on my heart, and I am glad
As I myself were there! Nor in this bower,
This little lime-tree bower, have I not mark'd
Much that has sooth'd me. Pale beneath the blaze
Hung the transparent foliage; and I watch'd
Some broad and sunny leaf, and lov'd to see
The shadow of the leaf and stem above
Dappling its sunshine! And that walnut-tree
Was richly ting'd, and a deep radiance lay
Full on the ancient ivy, which usurps
Those fronting elms, and now, with blackest mass
Makes their dark branches gleam a lighter hue
Through the late twilight: and though now the bat
Wheels silent by, and not a swallow twitters,
Yet still the solitary humble-bee
Sings in the bean-flower! Henceforth I shall know
That Nature ne'er deserts the wise and pure;

No plot so narrow, be but Nature there,
No waste so vacant, but may well employ
Each faculty of sense, and keep the heart
Awake to Love and Beauty! and sometimes
'Tis well to be bereft of promis'd good,
That we may lift the soul, and contemplate
With lively joy the joys we cannot share.
My gentle-hearted Charles! when the last rook
Beat its straight path along the dusky air
Homewards, I blest it! deeming its black wing
(Now a dim speck, now vanishing in light)
Had cross'd the mighty Orb's dilated glory,
While thou stood'st gazing; or, when all was still,
Flew creeking o'er thy head, and had a charm
For thee, my gentle-hearted Charles, to whom
No sound is dissonant which tells of Life.

Samuel Taylor Coleridge (1772–1834)

I Wandered Lonely as a Cloud

I wandered lonely as a cloud
That floats on high o'er vales and hills,
When all at once I saw a crowd,
A host, of golden daffodils;
Beside the lake, beneath the trees,
Fluttering and dancing in the breeze.

Continuous as the stars that shine
And twinkle on the milky way,
They stretched in never-ending line
Along the margin of a bay:
Ten thousand saw I at a glance,
Tossing their heads in sprightly dance.

The waves beside them danced; but they
Out-did the sparkling waves in glee:
A poet could not but be gay,
In such a jocund company:
I gazed – and gazed – but little thought
What wealth the show to me had brought:

For oft, when on my couch I lie
In vacant or in pensive mood,
They flash upon that inward eye
Which is the bliss of solitude;
And then my heart with pleasure fills,
And dances with the daffodils.

William Wordsworth (1770–1850)

Sudden Light

I have been here before,
But when or how I cannot tell:
I know the grass beyond the door,
The sweet keen smell,
The sighing sound, the lights around the shore.

You have been mine before, –
How long ago I may not know:
But just when at that swallow's soar
Your neck turn'd so,
Some veil did fall, – I knew it all of yore.

Has this been thus before?
And shall not thus time's eddying flight
Still with our lives our love restore
In death's despite,
And day and night yield one delight once more?

Dante Gabriel Rossetti (1828–1882)

from *Richard II*

This royal throne of kings, this sceptred isle,
This earth of majesty, this seat of Mars,
This other Eden, demi-paradise,
This fortress built by nature for herself
Against infection and the hand of war,
This happy breed of men, this little world,
This precious stone set in the silver sea,
Which serves it in the office of a wall,
Or as a moat defensive to a house
Against the envy of less happier lands;
This blessed plot, this earth, this realm, this
  England . . .

William Shakespeare (1564–1616)

A Strip of Blue

I do not own an inch of land,
    But all I see is mine, –
The orchard and the mowing fields,
    The lawns and gardens fine.
The winds my tax-collectors are,
    They bring me tithes divine, –
Wild scents and subtle essences,
    A tribute rare and free;
And, more magnificent than all,
    My window keeps for me
A glimpse of blue immensity, –
    A little strip of sea.

Richer am I than he who owns
    Great fleets and argosies;
I have a share in every ship
    Won by the inland breeze,
To loiter on yon airy road
    Above the apple-trees,
I freight them with my untold dreams;
    Each bears my own picked crew;
And nobler cargoes wait for them
    Than ever India knew, –
My ships that sail into the East
    Across that outlet blue.

Sometimes they seem like living shapes, –
    The people of the sky, –
Guests in white raiment coming down
    From heaven, which is close by;
I call them by familiar names,

As one by one draws nigh,
So white, so light, so spirit-like,
　　From violet mists they bloom!
The aching wastes of the unknown
　　Are half reclaimed from gloom,
Since on life's hospitable sea
　　All souls find sailing-room.

The ocean grows a weariness
　　With nothing else in sight;
Its east and west, its north and south,
　　Spread out from morn till night;
We miss the warm, caressing shore,
　　Its brooding shade and light.

Lucy Larcom (1824–1893)

WHERE GO THE BOATS?

Where go the Boats?

Dark brown is the river,
  Golden is the sand.
It flows along for ever,
  With trees on either hand.

Green leaves a-floating,
  Castles of the foam,
Boats of mine a-boating –
  Where will all come home?

On goes the river,
  And out past the mill,
Away down the valley,
  Away down the hill.

Away down the river,
  A hundred miles or more,
Other little children
  Shall bring my boats ashore.

Robert Louis Stevenson (1850–1894)

Seaweed

Seaweed sways and sways and swirls
as if swaying were its form of stillness;
and it flushes against fierce rock
it slips over it as shadows do, without hurting itself.

D. H. Lawrence (1885–1930)

O to sail

O to sail in a ship,
To leave this steady unendurable land,
To leave the tiresome sameness of the streets, the
    sidewalks and the houses,
To leave you, O you solid motionless land, and
    entering a ship,
To sail and sail and sail!

Walt Whitman (1819–1892)

Dover Beach

The sea is calm tonight.
The tide is full, the moon lies fair
Upon the straits; – on the French coast the light
Gleams and is gone; the cliffs of England stand,
Glimmering and vast, out in the tranquil bay.
Come to the window, sweet is the night-air!
Only, from the long line of spray
Where the sea meets the moon-blanched land,
Listen! you hear the grating roar
Of pebbles which the waves draw back, and fling,
At their return, up the high strand,
Begin, and cease, and then again begin,
With tremulous cadence slow, and bring
The eternal note of sadness in.

Sophocles long ago
Heard it on the Aegean, and brought
Into his mind the turbid ebb and flow
Of human misery; we
Find also in the sound a thought,
Hearing it by this distant northern sea.

The Sea of Faith
Was once, too, at the full, and round earth's shore
Lay like the folds of a bright girdle furled.
But now I only hear
Its melancholy, long, withdrawing roar,
Retreating, to the breath
Of the night-wind, down the vast edges drear
And naked shingles of the world.

Ah, love, let us be true
To one another! for the world, which seems
To lie before us like a land of dreams,
So various, so beautiful, so new,
Hath really neither joy, nor love, nor light,
Nor certitude, nor peace, nor help for pain;
And we are here as on a darkling plain
Swept with confused alarms of struggle and flight,
Where ignorant armies clash by night.

Matthew Arnold (1822–1888)

Ariel's Song

Full fathom five thy father lies,
   Of his bones are coral made:
Those are pearls that were his eyes,
   Nothing of him that doth fade,
But doth suffer a sea-change
Into something rich, and strange:
Sea-nymphs hourly ring his knell –
   Hark! now I hear them,
     Ding-dong bell.

William Shakespeare (1564–1616)

The Owl and the Pussy-Cat

The Owl and the Pussy-Cat went to sea
  In a beautiful pea-green boat,
They took some honey, and plenty of money,
  Wrapped up in a five-pound note.
The Owl looked up to the stars above,
  And sang to a small guitar,
'O lovely Pussy! O Pussy, my love,
    What a beautiful Pussy you are,
      You are,
      You are!
    What a beautiful Pussy you are!'

Pussy said to the Owl, 'You elegant fowl!
  How charmingly sweet you sing!
O let us be married! too long have we tarried:
  But what shall we do for a ring?'
They sailed away, for a year and a day,
  To the land where the Bong-tree grows,
And there in a wood a Piggy-wig stood
    With a ring at the end of his nose,
      His nose,
      His nose,
    With a ring at the end of his nose.

'Dear Pig, are you willing to sell for one shilling
  Your ring?' Said the Piggy, 'I will.'
So they took it away, and were married next day
  By the Turkey who lives on the hill.
They dined on mince, and slices of quince,
  Which they ate with a runcible spoon;

And hand in hand, on the edge of the sand,
   They danced by the light of the moon,
      The moon,
      The moon,
   They danced by the light of the moon.

Edward Lear (1812–1888)

I Was Born Upon Thy Bank, River

I was born upon thy bank, river,
  My blood flows in thy stream,
And thou meanderest forever
  At the bottom of my dream.

Henry David Thoreau (1817–1862)

from Childe Harold's Pilgrimage

Adieu, adieu! my native shore
       Fades o'er the waters blue;
The night-winds sigh, the breakers roar,
       And shrieks the wild sea-mew.
Yon sun that sets upon the sea
       We follow in his flight;
Farewell awhile to him and thee,
       My native Land – Good Night!

A few short hours, and he will rise
       To give the morrow birth;
And I shall hail the main and skies,
       But not my mother earth.
Deserted is my own good hall,
       Its hearth is desolate;
Wild weeds are gathering on the wall;
       My dog howls at the gate.

George Gordon, Lord Byron (1788–1824)

The Cataract of Lodore

'How does the water
Come down at Lodore?'
My little boy asked me
Thus, once on a time;
And moreover he tasked me
To tell him in rhyme.
Anon, at the word,
There first came one daughter,
And then came another,
To second and third
The request of their brother,
And to hear how the water
Comes down at Lodore,
With its rush and its roar,
As many a time
They had seen it before.
So I told them in rhyme,
For of rhymes I had store;
And 'twas in my vocation
For their recreation
That so I should sing;
Because I was Laureate
To them and the King.

From its sources which well
In the tarn on the fell;
From its fountains
In the mountains,
Its rills and its gills;
Through moss and through brake,
It runs and it creeps

For a while, till it sleeps
In its own little lake.
And thence at departing,
Awakening and starting,
It runs through the reeds,
And away it proceeds,
Through meadow and glade,
In sun and in shade,
And through the wood-shelter,
Among crags in its flurry,
Helter-skelter,
Hurry-skurry.
Here it comes sparkling,
And there it lies darkling;
Now smoking and frothing
Its tumult and wrath in,
Till, in this rapid race
On which it is bent,
It reaches the place
Of its steep descent.

The cataract strong
Then plunges along,
Striking and raging

As if a war raging
Its caverns and rocks among;
Rising and leaping,
Sinking and creeping,
Swelling and sweeping,
Showering and springing,
Flying and flinging,
Writhing and ringing,
Eddying and whisking,

Spouting and frisking,
Turning and twisting,
Around and around
With endless rebound:
Smiting and fighting,
A sight to delight in;
Confounding, astounding,
Dizzying and deafening the ear with its sound.

Collecting, projecting,
Receding and speeding,
And shocking and rocking,
And darting and parting,
And threading and spreading,
And whizzing and hissing,
And dripping and skipping,
And hitting and splitting,
And shining and twining,
And rattling and battling,
And shaking and quaking,
And pouring and roaring,
And waving and raving,
And tossing and crossing,
And flowing and going,
And running and stunning,
And foaming and roaming,
And dinning and spinning,
And dropping and hopping,
And working and jerking,
And guggling and struggling,
And heaving and cleaving,
And moaning and groaning;

And glittering and frittering,
And gathering and feathering,
And whitening and brightening,
And quivering and shivering,
And hurrying and skurrying,
And thundering and floundering;

Dividing and gliding and sliding,
And falling and brawling and sprawling,
And driving and riving and striving,
And sprinkling and twinkling and wrinkling,
And sounding and bounding and rounding,
And bubbling and troubling and doubling,
And grumbling and rumbling and tumbling,
And clattering and battering and shattering;

Retreating and beating and meeting and sheeting,
Delaying and straying and playing and spraying,
Advancing and prancing and glancing and dancing,
Recoiling, turmoiling and toiling and boiling,
And gleaming and streaming and steaming and
   beaming,
And rushing and flushing and brushing and gushing,
And flapping and rapping and clapping and slapping,
And curling and whirling and purling and twirling,
And thumping and plumping and bumping and
   jumping,
And dashing and flashing and splashing and clashing;
And so never ending, but always descending,
Sounds and motions for ever and ever are blending
All at once and all o'er, with a mighty uproar, –
And this way the water comes down at Lodore.

Robert Southey (1774–1843)

Exultation is in the Going

Exultation is in the going
Of an inland soul to sea,
Past the houses – past the headlands –
Into deep Eternity –

Bred as we, among the mountains,
Can the sailor understand
The divine intoxication
Of the first league out from land?

Emily Dickinson (1830–1886)

The Secret of the Sea

Ah! what pleasant visions haunt me
  As I gaze upon the sea!
All the old romantic legends,
  All my dreams, come back to me.

Sails of silk and ropes of sandal,
  Such as gleam in ancient lore;
And the singing of the sailors,
  And the answer from the shore!

Most of all, the Spanish ballad
  Haunts me oft, and tarries long,
Oft the noble Count Arnaldos
  And the sailor's mystic song.

Like the long waves on a sea-bench,
  Where the sand as silver shines,
With a soft, monotonous cadence,
  Flow its unrhymed lyric lines; –

Telling how the Count Arnaldos,
  With his hawk upon his hand,
Saw a fair and stately galley,
  Steering onward to the land; –

How he heard the ancient helmsman
  Chant a song so wild and clear,
That the sailing sea-bird slowly
  Poised upon the mast to hear,

Till his soul was full of longing,
    And he cried, with impulse strong, –
'Helmsman! for the love of heaven,
    Teach me, too, that wondrous song!'

'Wouldst thou,' – so the helmsman answered,
    'Learn the secret of the sea?
Only those who brave its dangers
    Comprehend its mystery!'

In each sail that skims the horizon,
    In each landward-blowing breeze,
I behold that stately galley,
    Hear those mournful melodies;

Till my soul is full of longing
    For the secret of the sea,
And the heart of the great ocean
    Sends a thrilling pulse through me.

Henry Wadsworth Longfellow (1807–1882)

In Cabin'd Ships At Sea

In cabin'd ships at sea,
The boundless blue on every side expanding,
With whistling winds and music of the waves, the
    large imperious waves,
Or some lone bark buoy'd on the dense marine,
Where joyous full of faith, spreading white sails,
She cleaves the ether mid the sparkle and the foam of
    day, or under many a star at night,
By sailors young and old haply will I, a reminiscence
    of the land, be read,
In full rapport at last.

Here are our thoughts, voyagers' thoughts.
Here not the land, firm land, alone appears, may then by
    them be said.
The sky o'erarches here, we feel the undulating deck
    beneath our feet,
We feel the long pulsation, ebb and flow of endless motion,
The tones of unseen mystery, the vague and vast
    suggestions of the briny world, the liquid-flowing
    syllables,
The perfume, the faint creaking of the cordage, the
    melancholy rhythm,
The boundless vista and the horizon far and dim are all
    here.
And this is ocean's poem.

Then falter not O book, fulfil your destiny,
You not a reminiscence of the land alone,
You too as a lone bark cleaving the ether, purpos'd I
    know not whither, yet ever full of faith,

Consort to every ship that sails, sail you!
Bear forth to them folded my love, (dear mariners, for
    you I fold it here in every leaf;)
Speed on my book! spread your white sails my little
    bark athwart the imperious waves,
Chant on, sail on, bear o'er the boundless blue from
    me to every sea,
The song for mariners and all their ships.

Walt Whitman (1819–1892)

Song

The boat is chafing at our long delay,
  And we must leave too soon
The spicy sea-pinks and the inborne spray,
  The tawny sands, the moon.

Keep us, O Thetis, in our western flight!
  Watch from thy pearly throne
Our vessel, plunging deeper into night
  To reach a land unknown.

John Davidson (1857–1909)

The Winds of Fate

One ship drives east and another drives west
    With the selfsame winds that blow.
        'Tis the set of the sails
        And not of the gales
    Which tells us the way to go.

Like the winds of the sea are the ways of fate,
    As we voyage along through life;
        'Tis the set of a soul
        That decides its goal,
    And not the calm or the strife.

Ella Wheeler Wilcox (1850–1919)

I Saw a Ship a-Sailing

I saw a ship a-sailing
A-sailing on the sea
And oh but it was laden
With lovely things for me

There were chocolates in the cabin
And ice cream in the hold
The sails were made of candyfloss
And the masts were all of gold

The four-and-twenty sailors
That stood between the decks
Were four-and-twenty white mice
With ribbons round their necks

The captain was a duck
With a parrot on his back
And when the mice were naughty
The captain said Quack! Quack!

Anon.

All Day I Hear the Noise of Waters

All day I hear the noise of waters
    Making moan,
Sad as the sea-bird is, when going
    Forth alone,
He hears the winds cry to the waters'
    Monotone.

The grey winds, the cold winds are blowing
    Where I go.
I hear the noise of many waters
    Far below.
All day, all night, I hear them flowing
    To and fro.

James Joyce (1882–1941)

'By lone St. Mary's silent lake'

By lone St. Mary's silent lake:
Thou know'st it well, – nor fen nor sedge
Pollute the pure lake's crystal edge;
Abrupt and sheer, the mountains sink
At once upon the level brink;
And just a trace of silver sand
Marks where the water meets the land.
Far in the mirror, bright and blue,
Each hill's huge outline you may view;
Shaggy with heath, but lonely bare,
Nor tree, nor bush, nor brake, is there,
Save where, of land, yon slender line
Bears thwart the lake the scatter'd pine.
Yet even this nakedness has power,
And aids the feeling of the hour:
Nor thicket, dell, nor copse you spy,
Where living thing concealed might lie;
Nor point, retiring, hides a dell,
Where swain, or woodman lone, might dwell;
There's nothing left to fancy's guess,
You see that all is loneliness:
And silence aids – though the steep hills
Send to the lake a thousand rills;
In summer tide, so soft they weep,
The sound but lulls the ear asleep;
Your horse's hoof-tread sounds too rude,
So stilly is the solitude.

Sir Walter Scott (1771–1832)

Anchored

If thro' the sea of night which
    here surrounds me,
  I could swim out beyond the
    farthest star,
Break every barrier of circumstance
    that bounds me,
  And greet the Sun of sweeter
    life afar,

Tho' near you there is passion,
    grief, and sorrow,
  And out there rest and joy and
    peace and all,
I should renounce that beckoning
    for to-morrow,
  I could not choose to go beyond
    your call.

Paul Laurence Dunbar (1876–1906)

The Tide Rises, the Tide Falls

The tide rises, the tide falls,
The twilight darkens, the curlew calls;
Along the sea-sands damp and brown
The traveller hastens toward the town,
    And the tide rises, the tide falls.

Darkness settles on roofs and walls,
But the sea, the sea in the darkness calls;
The little waves, with their soft, white hands,
Efface the footprints in the sands,
    And the tide rises, the tide falls.

The morning breaks; the steeds in their stalls
Stamp and neigh, as the hostler calls;
The day returns, but nevermore
Returns the traveller to the shore,
    And the tide rises, the tide falls.

Henry Wadsworth Longfellow (1807–1882)

Les Silhouettes

The sea is flecked with bars of grey,
The dull dead wind is out of tune,
And like a withered leaf the moon
Is blown across the stormy bay.

Etched clear upon the pallid sand
The black boat lies: a sailor boy
Clambers aboard in careless joy
With laughing face and gleaming hand.

And overhead the curlews cry,
Where through the dusky upland grass
The young brown-throated reapers pass,
Like silhouettes against the sky.

Oscar Wilde (1854–1900)

The Inchcape Rock

No stir in the air, no stir in the sea,
The Ship was still as she could be;
Her sails from heaven received no motion,
Her keel was steady in the ocean.

Without either sign or sound of their shock,
The waves flow'd over the Inchcape Rock;
So little they rose, so little they fell,
They did not move the Inchcape Bell.

The Abbot of Aberbrothok
Had placed that bell on the Inchcape Rock;
On a buoy in the storm it floated and swung,
And over the waves its warning rung.

When the Rock was hid by the surge's swell,
The Mariners heard the warning Bell;
And then they knew the perilous Rock,
And blest the Abbot of Aberbrothok.

The Sun in the heaven was shining gay,
All things were joyful on that day;
The sea-birds scream'd as they wheel'd round,
And there was joyaunce in their sound.

The buoy of the Inchcape Bell was seen
A darker speck on the ocean green;
Sir Ralph the Rover walk'd his deck,
And fix'd his eye on the darker speck.

He felt the cheering power of spring,
It made him whistle, it made him sing;
His heart was mirthful to excess,
But the Rover's mirth was wickedness.

His eye was on the Inchcape Float;
Quoth he, 'My men, put out the boat,
And row me to the Inchcape Rock,
And I'll plague the Abbot of Aberbrothok.'

The boat is lower'd, the boatmen row,
And to the Inchcape Rock they go;
Sir Ralph bent over from the boat,
And he cut the Bell from the Inchcape Float.

Down sank the Bell with a gurgling sound,
The bubbles rose and burst around;
Quoth Sir Ralph, 'The next who comes to the Rock,
Won't bless the Abbot of Aberbrothok.'

Sir Ralph the Rover sail'd away,
He scour'd the seas for many a day;
And now grown rich with plunder'd store,
He steers his course for Scotland's shore.

So thick a haze o'erspreads the sky,
They cannot see the sun on high;
The wind hath blown a gale all day,
At evening it hath died away.

On the deck the Rover takes his stand,
So dark it is they see no land.
Quoth Sir Ralph, 'It will be lighter soon,
For there is the dawn of the rising Moon.'

'Canst hear,' said one, 'the breakers roar?
For methinks we should be near the shore.'
'Now, where we are I cannot tell,
But I wish we could hear the Inchcape Bell.'

They hear no sound, the swell is strong,
Though the wind hath fallen they drift along;
Till the vessel strikes with a shivering shock,
'Oh Christ! It is the Inchcape Rock!'

Sir Ralph the Rover tore his hair,
He curst himself in his despair;
The waves rush in on every side,
The ship is sinking beneath the tide.

But even in his dying fear,
One dreadful sound could the Rover hear;
A sound as if with the Inchcape Bell,
The Devil below was ringing his knell.

Robert Southey (1774–1843)

Possibilities

Where are the poets, unto whom belong
  The Olympian heights; whose singing shafts were sent
  Straight to the mark, and not from bows half bent,
  But with the utmost tension of the thong?
Where are the stately argosies of song,
  Whose rushing keels made music as they went
  Sailing in search of some new continent,
  With all sail set, and steady winds and strong?
Perhaps there lives some dreamy boy, untaught
  In schools, some graduate of the field or street,
An admiral sailing the high seas of thought,
  Fearless and first, and steering with his fleet
  For lands not yet laid down in any chart.

Henry Wadsworth Longfellow (1807–1882)

The Flying Dutchman

Unyielding in the pride of his defiance,
  Afloat with none to serve or to command,
Lord of himself at last, and all by Science,
  He seeks the Vanished Land.

Alone, by the one light of his one thought,
  He steers to find the shore from which we came,
Fearless of in what coil he may be caught
  On seas that have no name.

Into the night he sails; and after night
  There is a dawning, though there be no sun;
Wherefore, with nothing but himself in sight,
  Unsighted, he sails on.

At last there is a lifting of the cloud
  Between the flood before him and the sky;
And then – though he may curse the Power aloud
  That has no power to die –

He steers himself away from what is haunted
  By the old ghost of what has been before, –
Abandoning, as always, and undaunted,
  One fog-walled island more.

Edwin Arlington Robinson (1869–1935)

Ships That Pass in the Night

Out in the sky the great dark clouds are massing;
   I look far out into the pregnant night,
Where I can hear a solemn booming gun
   And catch the gleaming of a random light,
That tells me that the ship I seek is passing, passing.

My tearful eyes my soul's deep hurt are glassing;
   For I would hail and check that ship of ships.
I stretch my hands imploring, cry aloud,
   My voice falls dead a foot from mine own lips,
And but its ghost doth reach that vessel, passing,
   passing.

O Earth, O Sky, O Ocean, both surpassing,
   O heart of mine, O soul that dreads the dark!
Is there no hope for me? Is there no way
   That I may sight and check that speeding bark
Which out of sight and sound is passing, passing?

Paul Laurence Dunbar (1876–1906)

There Is No Frigate Like a Book

There is no Frigate like a Book
To take us Lands away,
Nor any Coursers like a Page
Of prancing Poetry –
This Travel may the poorest take
Without offense of Toll –
How frugal is the Chariot
That bears the Human soul.

Emily Dickinson (1830–1886)

Emigravit

With sails full set, the ship her anchor weighs.
Strange names shine out beneath her figure head.
What glad farewells with eager eyes are said!
What cheer for him who goes, and him who stays!
Fair skies, rich lands, new homes, and untried days
Some go to seek: the rest but wait instead,
Watching the way wherein their comrades led,
Until the next stanch ship her flag doth raise.
Who knows what myriad colonies there are
Of fairest fields, and rich, undreamed-of gains
Thick planted in the distant shining plains
Which we call sky because they lie so far?
Oh, write of me, not 'Died in bitter pains,'
But 'Emigrated to another star!'

Helen Hunt Jackson (1830–1885)

from Don Juan

V

The wind swept down the Euxine, and the wave
  Broke foaming o'er the blue Symplegades;
'Tis a grand sight from off the 'Giant's Grave'
  To watch the progress of those rolling seas
Between the Bosphorus, as they lash and lave
  Europe and Asia, you being quite at ease;
There's not a sea the passenger e'er pukes in,
  Turns up more dangerous breakers than the Euxine.

George Gordon, Lord Byron (1788–1824)

DEPARTURE PLATFORM

Departure Platform

We kissed at the barrier; and passing through
She left me, and moment by moment got
Smaller and smaller, until to my view
      She was but a spot;

A wee white spot of muslin fluff
That down the diminishing platform bore
Through hustling crowds of gentle and rough
      To the carriage door.

Under the lamplight's fitful glowers,
Behind dark groups from far and near,
Whose interests were apart from ours,
      She would disappear,

Then show again, till I ceased to see
That flexible form, that nebulous white;
And she who was more than my life to me
      Had vanished quite.

We have penned new plans since that fair fond day,
And in season she will appear again –
Perhaps in the same soft white array –
      But never as then!

– 'And why, young man, must eternally fly
A joy you'll repeat, if you love her well?'
– O friend, nought happens twice thus; why,
      I cannot tell!

Thomas Hardy (1840–1928)

From a Railway Carriage

Faster than fairies, faster than witches,
Bridges and houses, hedges and ditches;
And charging along like troops in a battle,
All through the meadows the horses and cattle:
All of the sights of the hill and the plain
Fly as thick as driving rain;
And ever again, in the wink of an eye,
Painted stations whistle by.

Here is a child who clambers and scrambles,
All by himself and gathering brambles;
Here is a tramp who stands and gazes;
And there is the green for stringing the daisies!
Here is a cart run away in the road
Lumping along with man and load;
And here is a mill and there is a river:
Each a glimpse and gone for ever!

Robert Louis Stevenson (1850–1894)

To a Locomotive in Winter

Thee for my recitative,
Thee in the driving storm even as now, the snow, the
    winter-day declining,
Thee in thy panoply, thy measur'd dual throbbing and
    thy beat convulsive,
Thy black cylindric body, golden brass and silvery
    steel,
Thy ponderous side-bars, parallel and connecting
    rods, gyrating, shuttling at thy sides,
Thy metrical, now swelling pant and roar, now
    tapering in the distance,
Thy great protruding head-light fix'd in front,
Thy long, pale, floating vapor-pennants, tinged with
    delicate purple,
The dense and murky clouds out-belching from thy
    smoke-stack,
Thy knitted frame, thy springs and valves, the
    tremulous twinkle of thy wheels,
Thy train of cars behind, obedient, merrily following,
Through gale or calm, now swift, now slack, yet
    steadily careering;
Type of the modern – emblem of motion and
    power – pulse of the continent,
For once come serve the Muse and merge in verse,
    even as here I see thee,
With storm and buffeting gusts of wind and falling
    snow,
By day thy warning ringing bell to sound its notes,
By night thy silent signal lamps to swing.

Fierce-throated beauty!
Roll through my chant with all thy lawless music, thy
     swinging lamps at night,
Thy madly-whistled laughter, echoing, rumbling like
     an earthquake, rousing all,
Law of thyself complete, thine own track firmly
     holding
(No sweetness debonair of tearful harp or glib piano
     thine,)
Thy trills of shrieks by rocks and hills return'd,
Launch'd o'er the prairies wide, across the lakes,
To the free skies unspent and glad and strong.

Walt Whitman (1819–1892)

Midnight on the Great Western

In the third-class sat the journeying boy,
    And the roof-lamp's oily flame
Played down on his listless form and face,
Bewrapt past knowing to what he was going,
    Or whence he came.

In the band of his hat the journeying boy
    Had a ticket stuck; and a string
Around his neck bore the key of his box,
That twinkled gleams of the lamp's sad beams
    Like a living thing.

What past can be yours, O journeying boy,
    Towards a world unknown,
Who calmly, as if incurious quite
On all at stake, can undertake
    This plunge alone?

Knows your soul a sphere, O journeying boy,
    Our rude realms far above,
Whence with spacious vision you mark and mete
This region of sin that you find you in
    But are not of?

Thomas Hardy (1840–1928)

Taking the Night-Train

A tremulous word, a lingering hand, the burning
　Of restless passion smoldering – so we part;
Ah, slowly from the dark the world is turning
　When midnight stars shine in a heavy heart.

The streets are lighted, and the myriad faces
　Move through the gaslight, and the homesick feet
Pass by me, homeless; sweet and close embraces
　Charm many a threshold – laughs and kisses sweet.

From great hotels the stranger throng is streaming,
　The hurrying wheels in many a street are loud;
Within the depot, in the gaslight gleaming,
　A glare of faces, stands the waiting crowd.

The whistle screams; the wheels are rumbling slowly,
　The path before us glides into the light:
Behind, the city sinks in silence wholly;
　The panting engine leaps into the night.

I seem to see each street a mystery growing,
　In mist of dreamland – vague, forgotten air:
Does no sweet soul, awakened, feel me going?
　Loves no dear heart, in dreams, to keep me there?

John James Piatt (1835–1917)

The Night Journey

Hands and lit faces eddy to a line;
The dazed last minutes click; the clamour dies.
Beyond the great-swung arc o' the roof, divine,
Night, smoky-scarv'd, with thousand coloured eyes

Glares the imperious mystery of the way.
Thirsty for dark, you feel the long-limbed train
Throb, stretch, thrill motion, slide, pull out and sway,
Strain for the far, pause, draw to strength again . . .

As a man, caught by some great hour, will rise,
Slow-limbed, to meet the light or find his love;
And, breathing long, with staring sightless eyes,
Hands out, head back, agape and silent, move

Sure as a flood, smooth as a vast wind blowing;
And, gathering power and purpose as he goes,
Unstumbling, unreluctant, strong, unknowing,
Borne by a will not his, that lifts, that grows,

Sweep out to darkness, triumphing in his goal,
Out of the fire, out of the little room . . .
– There is an end appointed, O my soul!
Crimson and green the signals burn; the gloom

Is hung with steam's far-blowing livid streamers.
Lost into God, as lights in light, we fly,
Grown one with will, end-drunken huddled dreamers.
The white lights roar. The sounds of the world die.

And lips and laughter are forgotten things.
Speed sharpens; grows. Into the night, and on,
The strength and splendour of our purpose swings.
The lamps fade; and the stars. We are alone.

Rupert Brooke (1887–1915)

I like to see it lap the Miles

I like to see it lap the miles,
And lick the valleys up,
And stop to feed itself at tanks;
And then, prodigious, step

Around a pile of mountains,
And, supercilious, peer
In shanties by the sides of roads;
And then a quarry pare

To fit its sides, and crawl between,
Complaining all the while
In horrid, hooting stanza;
Then chase itself down hill

And neigh like Boanerges;
Then, punctual as a star,
Stop – docile and omnipotent –
At its own stable door.

Emily Dickinson (1830–1886)

The Engine

Into a gloom of the deep, dark night,
  With panting breath and a startled scream;
Swift as a bird in sudden flight
  Darts this creature of steel and steam.

Awful dangers are lurking nigh,
  Rocks and chasms are near the track,
But straight by the light of its great white eye
  It speeds through the shadows, dense and black.

Terrible thoughts and fierce desires
  Trouble its mad heart many an hour,
Where burn and smolder the hidden fires,
  Coupled ever with might and power.

It hates, as a wild horse hates the rein,
  The narrow track by vale and hill;
And shrieks with a cry of startled pain,
  And longs to follow its own wild will.

Ella Wheeler Wilcox (1850–1919)

HIGH FLIGHT

High Flight

Oh, I have slipped the surly bonds of earth,
And danced the skies on laughter-silvered wings;
Sunward I've climbed and joined the tumbling mirth
Of sun-split clouds – and done a hundred things
You have not dreamed of – wheeled and soared and
    swung
High in the sunlit silence. Hov'ring there
I've chased the shouting wind along and flung
My eager craft through footless halls of air.
Up, up the long delirious burning blue
I've topped the wind-swept heights with easy grace,
Where never lark, or even eagle, flew;
And, while with silent, lifting mind I've trod
The high untrespassed sanctity of space,
Put out my hand, and touched the face of God.

John Gillespie Magee, Jr. (1922–1941)

To a Waterfowl

Whither, 'midst falling dew,
   While glow the heavens with the last steps of day,
Far, through their rosy depths, dost thou pursue
   Thy solitary way?

Vainly the fowler's eye
   Might mark thy distant flight to do thee wrong,
As, darkly painted on the crimson sky,
   Thy figure floats along.

Seek'st thou the plashy brink
   Of weedy lake, or marge of river wide,
Or where the rocking billows rise and sink
   On the chafed ocean's side?

There is a Power whose care
   Teaches thy way along that pathless coast –
The desert and illimitable air –
   Lone wandering, but not lost.

All day thy wings have fanned,
   At that far height, the cold, thin atmosphere,
Yet stoop not weary, to the welcome land,
   Though the dark night is near.

And soon that toil shall end;
   Soon shalt thou find a summer home, and rest,
And scream among thy fellows; reeds shall bend,
   Soon, o'er thy sheltered nest.

Thou'rt gone! the abyss of heaven
   Hath swallowed up thy form; yet on my heart
Deeply hath sunk the lesson thou hast given,
   And shall not soon depart.

He who, from zone to zone,
   Guides through the boundless sky thy certain flight,
In the long way that I must tread alone
   Will lead my steps aright.

William Cullen Bryant (1794–1878)

Sympathy

I know what the caged bird feels, alas!
When the sun is bright on the upland slopes;
When the wind stirs soft through the springing grass
And the river flows like a stream of glass;
When the first bird sings and the first bud opes,
And the faint perfume from its chalice steals –
I know what the caged bird feels!

I know why the caged bird beats his wing
Till its blood is red on the cruel bars;
For he must fly back to his perch and cling
When he fain would be on the bough a-swing;
And a pain still throbs in the old, old scars
And they pulse again with a keener sting –
I know why he beats his wing!

I know why the caged bird sings, ah me,
When his wing is bruised and his bosom sore, –
When he beats his bars and would be free;
It is not a carol of joy or glee,
But a prayer that he sends from his deep heart's core,
But a plea, that upward to Heaven he flings –
I know why the caged bird sings!

Paul Laurence Dunbar (1876–1906)

To the Man-of-War Bird

Thou who hast slept all night upon the storm,
Waking renew'd on thy prodigious pinions,
(Burst the wild storm? above it thou ascend'st,
And rested on the sky, thy slave that cradled thee,)
Now a blue point, far, far in heaven floating,
As to the light emerging here on deck I watch thee,
(Myself a speck, a point on the world's floating vast.)
Far, far at sea,
After the night's fierce drifts have strewn the shore
    with wrecks,
With re-appearing day as now so happy and serene,
The rosy and elastic dawn, the flashing sun,
The limpid spread of air cerulean,
Thou also re-appearest.

Thou born to match the gale, (thou art all wings,)
To cope with heaven and earth and sea and hurricane,
Thou ship of air that never furl'st thy sails,
Days, even weeks untired and onward, through
    spaces, realms gyrating
At dusk that look'st on Senegal, at morn America,
That sport'st amid the lightning-flash and
    thunder-cloud,
In them, in thy experiences, had'st thou my soul,
What joys! What joys were thine!

Walt Whitman (1819–1892)

When I Heard the Learn'd Astronomer

When I heard the learn'd astronomer,
When the proofs, the figures, were ranged in columns
    before me,
When I was shown the charts and diagrams, to add,
    divide, and measure them,
When I sitting heard the astronomer where he
    lectured with much applause in the lecture-room,
How soon unaccountable I became tired and sick,
Till rising and gliding out I wander'd off by myself,
In the mystical moist night-air, and from time to time,
Look'd up in perfect silence at the stars.

Walt Whitman (1819–1892)

BEAUTIFUL CITY

Beautiful City

Beautiful city, the centre and crater of European
    confusion,
O you with your passionate shriek for the rights of an
    equal humanity,
How often your Re-volution has proven but
    E-volution
Roll'd again back on itself in the tides of a civic
    insanity!

Alfred, Lord Tennyson (1809–1892)

Composed Upon Westminster Bridge

Earth has not anything to show more fair:
Dull would he be of soul who could pass by
A sight so touching in its majesty:
This City now doth, like a garment, wear
The beauty of the morning; silent, bare,
Ships, towers, domes, theatres, and temples lie
Open unto the fields, and to the sky;
All bright and glittering in the smokeless air.
Never did sun more beautifully steep
In his first splendour, valley, rock, or hill;
Ne'er saw I, never felt, a calm so deep!
The river glideth at his own sweet will:
Dear God! the very houses seem asleep;
And all that mighty heart is lying still!

William Wordsworth (1770–1850)

from The Earthly Paradise

Forget six counties overhung with smoke,
Forget the snorting steam and piston stroke,
Forget the spreading of the hideous town;
Think rather of the pack-horse on the down,
And dream of London, small and white, and clean,
The clear Thames bordered by its gardens green.

William Morris (1834–1896)

Twickenham Garden

Blasted with sighs, and surrounded with teares,
  Hither I come to seeke the spring,
  And at mine eyes, and at mine eares,
Recieve such balmes, as else cure every thing;
  But O, selfe traytor, I do bring
The spider love, which transubstantiates all,
  And can convert Manna to gall,
And that this place may thoroughly be thought
  True Paradise, I have the serpent brought.

'Twere wholsomer for mee, that winter did
  Benight the glory of this place,
  And that a grave frost did forbid
These trees to laugh, and mocke mee to my face;
  But that I may not this disgrace
Indure, nor yet leave loving, Love let mee
  Some senslesse peece of this place bee;
Make me a mandrake, so I may groane here,
  Or a stone fountain weeping out my yeare.

Hither with christall vyals, lovers come,
  And take my teares, which are loves wine,
  And try your mistresse Teares at home,
For all are false, that tast not just like mine;
  Alas, hearts do not in eyes shine,
Nor can you more judge womans thoughts by teares,
  Than by her shadow, what she weares.
O perverse sexe, where none is true but shee,
  Who's therefore true, because her truth kills mee.

John Donne (c.1572–1631)

The Fire of London

from Annus Mirabilis: The Year of Wonders, verses 215–18

Such was the Rise of the prodigious fire,
Which in mean Buildings first obscurely bred,
From thence did soon to open Streets aspire,
And straight to Palaces and Temples spread.

The diligence of Trades and noiseful Gain,
And luxury, more late, asleep were laid:
All was the nights, and in her silent reign
No sound the rest of Nature did invade.

In this deep quiet, from what source unknown,
Those seeds of Fire their fatal Birth disclose;
And first, few scatt'ring Sparks about were blown,
Big with the flames that to our Ruin rose.

Then, in some close-pent Room it crept along,
And, smouldering as it went, in silence fed;
Till th'infant Monster, with devouring strong,
Walk'd boldly upright with exalted head.

John Dryden (1631–1700)

Oranges and Lemons

Oranges and lemons,
Say the bells of St. Clement's.

You owe me five farthings,
Say the bells of St. Martin's.

When will you pay me?
Say the bells of Old Bailey.

When I grow rich,
Say the bells of Shoreditch.

When will that be?
Say the bells of Stepney.

I do not know,
Says the great bell at Bow.

Here comes a candle to light you to bed,
Here comes a chopper to chop off your head!

Anon.

Easter Day

The silver trumpets rang across the Dome:
  The people knelt upon the ground with awe:
  And borne upon the necks of men I saw,
Like some great God, the Holy Lord of Rome.
Priest-like, he wore a robe more white than foam,
  And, king-like, swathed himself in royal red,
  Three crowns of gold rose high upon his head:
In splendour and in light the Pope passed home.
My heart stole back across wide wastes of years
  To One who wandered by a lonely sea,
  And sought in vain for any place of rest:
'Foxes have holes, and every bird its nest,
I, only I, must wander wearily,
And bruise My feet, and drink wine salt with tears.'

Oscar Wilde (1854–1900)

Place De La Bastille

How dear the sky has been above this place!
Small treasures of this sky that we see here
Seen weak through prison-bars from year to year;
Eyed with a painful prayer upon God's grace
To save, and tears which stayed along the face
Lifted at sunset. Yea, how passing dear
Those nights when through the bars a wind left clear
The heaven, and moonlight soothed the limpid space!
So was it, till one night the secret kept
Safe in low vault and stealthy corridor
Was blown abroad on gospel-tongues of flame.
O ways of God, mysterious evermore!
How many on this spot have cursed and wept
That all might stand here now and own Thy Name.

Dante Gabriel Rossetti (1828–1882)

Paris in Spring

The city's all a-shining
Beneath a fickle sun,
A gay young wind's a-blowing,
The little shower is done.
But the rain-drops still are clinging
And falling one by one –
Oh it's Paris, it's Paris,
And spring-time has begun.

I know the Bois is twinkling
In a sort of hazy sheen,
And down the Champs the gray old arch
Stands cold and still between.
But the walk is flecked with sunlight
Where the great acacias lean,
Oh it's Paris, it's Paris,
And the leaves are growing green.

The sun's gone in, the sparkle's dead,
There falls a dash of rain,
But who would care when such an air
Comes blowing up the Seine?
And still Ninette sits sewing
Beside her window-pane,
When it's Paris, it's Paris,
And spring-time's come again.

Sara Teasdale (1884–1933)

The City's Love

For one brief golden moment rare like wine,
The gracious city swept across the line;
Oblivious of the color of my skin,
Forgetting that I was an alien guest,
She bent to me, my hostile heart to win,
Caught me in passion to her pillowy breast.
The great, proud city, seized with a strange love,
Bowed down for one flame hour my pride to prove.

Claude McKay (1889–1948)

America for Me

'Tis fine to see the Old World, and travel up and down
Among the famous palaces and cities of renown,
To admire the crumbly castles and the statues of the
    kings, –
But now I think I've had enough of antiquated things.

So it's home again, and home again, America for me!
My heart is turning home again, and there I long to be,
In the land of youth and freedom beyond the ocean bars,
Where the air is full of sunlight and the flag is full of stars.

Oh, London is a man's town, there's power in the air;
And Paris is a woman's town, with flowers in her hair;
And it's sweet to dream in Venice, and it's great to
    study Rome;
But when it comes to living there is no place like
    home.

I like the German fir-woods, in green battalions drilled;
I like the gardens of Versailles with flashing fountains
    filled;
But, oh, to take your hand, my dear, and ramble for
    a day
In the friendly western woodland where Nature has
    her way!

I know that Europe's wonderful, yet something seems
    to lack:
The Past is too much with her, and the people
    looking back.

But the glory of the Present is to make the Future
    free, –
We love our land for what she is and what she is to be.

Oh, it's home again, and home again, America for me!
I want a ship that's westward bound to plough the
    rolling sea,
To the blessed Land of Room Enough beyond the ocean
    bars,
Where the air is full of sunlight and the flag is full of stars.

                Henry Van Dyke (1852–1933)

The Harbor Dawn

Insistently through sleep – a tide of voices –
They meet you listening midway in your dream,
The long, tired sounds, fog-insulated noises:
Gongs in white surplices, beshrouded wails,
Far strum of fog horns ... signals dispersed in veils.

And then a truck will lumber past the wharves
As winch engines begin throbbing on some deck;
Or a drunken stevedore's howl and thud below
Comes echoing alley-upward through dim snow.

And if they take your sleep away sometimes
They give it back again. Soft sleeves of sound
Attend the darkling harbor, the pillowed bay;
Somewhere out there in blankness steam

Spills into stream, and wanders, washed away
– Flurried by keen fifings, eddied
Among distant chiming buoys – adrift. The sky,
Cool feathery fold, suspends, distils
This wavering slumber ... Slowly –
Immemorially the window, the half-covered chair
Ask nothing but this sheath of pallid air.

And you beside me, blessèd now while sirens
Sing to us, stealthily weave us into day –
Serenely now, before day claims our eyes
Your cool arms murmurously about me lay.

While myriad snowy hands are clustering at the panes –
    your hands within my hands are deeds;
    my tongue upon your throat – singing
    arms close; eyes wide, undoubtful
               dark
                      drink the dawn –
    a forest shudders in your hair!

The window goes blond slowly. Frostily clears.
From Cyclopean towers across Manhattan waters
– Two – three bright window-eyes aglitter, disk
The sun, released – aloft with cold gulls hither.

The fog leans one last moment on the sill.
Under the mistletoe of dreams, a star –
As though to join us at some distant hill –
Turns in the waking west and goes to sleep.

Hart Crane (1899–1932)

from Crossing Brooklyn Ferry

I

Flood-tide below me! I see you face to face!
Clouds of the west – sun there half an hour high –
    I see you also face to face.

Crowds of men and women attired in the usual
    costumes, how curious you are to me!
On the ferry-boats the hundreds and hundreds that
    cross, returning home, are more curious to me
    than you suppose,
And you that shall cross from shore to shore years
    hence are more to me, and more in my
    meditations, than you might suppose.

Walt Whitman (1819–1892)

To Brooklyn Bridge

How many dawns, chill from his rippling rest
The seagull's wings shall dip and pivot him,
Shedding white rings of tumult, building high
Over the chained bay waters Liberty –

Then, with inviolate curve, forsake our eyes
As apparitional as sails that cross
Some page of figures to be filed away:
– Till elevators drop us from our day . . .

I think of cinemas, panoramic sleights
With multitudes bent toward some flashing scene
Never disclosed, but hastened to again,
Foretold to other eyes on the same screen;

And Thee, across the harbor, silver-paced
As though the sun took step of thee, yet left
Some motion ever unspent in thy stride, –
Implicitly thy freedom staying thee!

Out of some subway scuttle, cell or loft
A bedlamite speeds to thy parapets,
Tilting there momently, shrill shirt ballooning,
A jest falls from the speechless caravan.

Down Wall, from girder into street noon leaks,
A rip-tooth of the sky's acetylene;
All afternoon the cloud-flown derricks turn . . .
Thy cables breathe the North Atlantic still.

And obscure as that heaven of the Jews,
Thy guerdon ... Accolade thou dost bestow
Of anonymity time cannot raise:
Vibrant reprieve and pardon thou dost show.

O harp and altar, of the fury fused,
(How could mere toil align thy choiring strings!)
Terrific threshold of the prophet's pledge,
Prayer of pariah, and the lover's cry, –

Again the traffic lights that skim thy swift
Unfractioned idiom, immaculate sigh of stars,
Beading thy path – condense eternity:
And we have seen night lifted in thine arms.

Under thy shadow by the piers I waited;
Only in darkness is thy shadow clear.
The City's fiery parcels all undone,
Already snow submerges an iron year ...

O Sleepless as the river under thee,
Vaulting the sea, the prairies' dreaming sod,
Unto us lowliest sometime sweep, descend
And of the curveship lend a myth to God.

Hart Crane (1899–1932)

Mannahatta

I was asking for something specific and perfect for
    my city
Whereupon lo! upsprang the aboriginal name.
Now I see what there is in a name, a word, liquid,
    sane, unruly, musical, self-sufficient,
I see that the word of my city is that word from of
    old,
Because I see that word nested in nests of water-bays,
    superb,
Rich, hemm'd thick all around with sailships and
    steamships, an island sixteen miles long,
    solid-founded,
Numberless crowded streets, high growths of iron,
    slender, strong, light, splendidly uprising toward
    clear skies,
Tides swift and ample, well-loved by me, toward
    sundown,
The flowing sea-currents, the little islands, larger
    adjoining islands, the heights, the villas,
The countless masts, the white shore-steamers, the
    lighters, the ferry-boats, the black sea-steamers
    well-model'd,
The down-town streets, the jobbers' houses of
    business, the houses of business of the ship-
    merchants and money-brokers, the river-streets,
Immigrants arriving, fifteen or twenty thousand in a
    week,
The carts hauling goods, the manly race of drivers of
    horses, the brown-faced sailors,
The summer air, the bright sun shining, and the
    sailing clouds aloft,

The winter snows, the sleigh-bells, the broken ice in
the river, passing along up or down with the
flood-tide or ebb-tide,
The mechanics of the city, the masters, well-form'd,
beautiful-faced, looking you straight in the eyes,
Trottoirs throng'd, vehicles, Broadway, the women,
the shops and shows,
A million people – manners free and superb – open
voices – hospitality – the most courageous and
friendly young men,
City of hurried and sparkling waters! city of spires
and masts!
City nested in bays! my city!

Walt Whitman (1819–1892)

The Taxi

When I am away from you
The world beats dead
Like a slackened drum
I call out for you against the jutted stars
And shout into the ridges of the wind.
Streets coming fast,
One after the other,
Wedge you away from me,
And the lamps of the city prick my eyes
So that I can no longer see your face.
Why should I leave you,
To wound myself upon the sharp edges of the night?

Amy Lowell (1874–1925)

Broadway

This is the quiet hour; the theaters
  Have gathered in their crowds, and steadily
  The million lights blaze on for few to see,
Robbing the sky of stars that should be hers.
A woman waits with bag and shabby furs,
  A somber man drifts by, and only we
  Pass up the street unwearied, warm and free,
For over us the olden magic stirs.
Beneath the liquid splendor of the lights
  We live a little ere the charm is spent;
This night is ours, of all the golden nights,
    The pavement an enchanted palace floor,
  And Youth the player on the viol, who sent
  A strain of music thru an open door.

Sara Teasdale (1884–1933)

Broadway

What hurrying human tides, or day or night!
What passions, winnings, losses, ardors, swim thy
    waters!
What whirls of evil, bliss and sorrow, stem thee!
What curious questioning glances – glints of love!
Leer, envy, scorn, contempt, hope, aspiration!
Thou portal – thou arena – thou of the myriad
    long-drawn lines and groups!
(Could but thy flagstones, curbs, façades, tell their
    inimitable tales;
Thy windows rich, and huge hotels – thy side-walks
    wide;)
Thou of the endless sliding, mincing, shuffling feet!
Thou, like the parti-colored world itself – like infinite,
    teeming, mocking life!
Thou visor'd, vast, unspeakable show and lesson!

Walt Whitman (1819–1892)

Union Square

With the man I love who loves me not,
  I walked in the street-lamps' flare;
We watched the world go home that night
  In a flood through Union Square.

I leaned to catch the words he said
  That were light as a snowflake falling;
Ah well that he never leaned to hear
  The words my heart was calling.

And on we walked and on we walked
  Past the fiery lights of the picture shows –
Where the girls with thirsty eyes go by
  On the errand each man knows.

And on we walked and on we walked,
  At the door at last we said good-bye;
I knew by his smile he had not heard
  My heart's unuttered cry.

With the man I love who loves me not
  I walked in the street-lamps' flare –
But oh, the girls who can ask for love
  In the lights of Union Square.

Sara Teasdale (1884–1933)

The Tropics in New York

Bananas ripe and green, and ginger-root,
  Cocoa in pods and alligator pears,
And tangerines and mangoes and grape fruit,
  Fit for the highest prize at parish fairs,

Set in the window, bringing memories
  Of fruit-trees laden by low-singing rills,
And dewy dawns, and mystical blue skies
  In benediction over nun-like hills.

My eyes grew dim, and I could no more gaze;
  A wave of longing through my body swept,
And, hungry for the old, familiar ways,
  I turned aside and bowed my head and wept.

Claude McKay (1889–1948)

The New Colossus

Not like the brazen giant of Greek fame,
With conquering limbs astride from land to land;
Here at our sea-washed, sunset gates shall stand
A mighty woman with a torch, whose flame
Is the imprisoned lightning, and her name
Mother of Exiles. From her beacon-hand
Glows world-wide welcome; her mild eyes command
The air-bridged harbor that twin cities frame.
'Keep, ancient lands, your storied pomp!' cries she
With silent lips. 'Give me your tired, your poor,
Your huddled masses yearning to breathe free,
The wretched refuse of your teeming shore.
Send these, the homeless, tempest-tost to me,
I lift my lamp beside the golden door!'

Emma Lazarus (1849–1887)

HOME, SWEET HOME

Home, Sweet Home!

'Mid pleasures and palaces though we may roam,
Be it ever so humble, there's no place like home.
A charm from the sky seems to hallow us there,
Which, seek through the world, is ne'er met with
    elsewhere.
        Home! sweet home!
        There's no place like home!

An exile from home, splendour dazzles in vain!
Oh! give me my lowly thatch'd cottage again!
The birds singing gaily that came at my call,
Give me them, with the peace of mind DEARER
    than all!
        Home! sweet home!
        There's no place like home!

John Howard Payne (1791–1852)

Home

How brightly glistening in the sun
  The woodland ivy plays!
While yonder beeches from their barks
  Reflect his silver rays.

That sun surveys a lovely scene
  From softly smiling skies;
And wildly through unnumbered trees
  The wind of winter sighs:

Now loud, it thunders o'er my head,
  And now in distance dies.
But give me back my barren hills
  Where colder breezes rise;

Where scarce the scattered, stunted trees
  Can yield an answered swell,
But where a wilderness of heath
  Returns the sound as well.

For yonder garden, fair and wide,
  With groves of evergreen,
Long winding walks, and borders trim,
  And velvet lawns between;

Restore to me that little spot,
  With grey walls compassed round,
Where knotted grass neglected lies,
  And weeds usurp the ground.

Though all around this mansion high
  Invites the foot to roam,
And though its halls are fair within –
  Oh, give me back my HOME!

Anne Brontë (1820–1849)

No Man is an Island

No man is an island,
entire of itself;
every man is a piece of the continent,
a part of the main.
If a clod be washed away by the sea,
Europe is the less,
as well as if a promontory were,
as well as if a manor of thy friend's
or of thine own were.
Any man's death diminishes me,
because I am involved in mankind;
and therefore never send to know for whom the bell
    tolls;
it tolls for thee.

John Donne (c.1572–1631)

Sonnet 50

How heavy do I journey on the way,
When what I seek, my weary travel's end,
Doth teach that ease and that repose to say,
'Thus far the miles are measured from thy friend!'
The beast that bears me, tired with my woe,
Plods dully on, to bear that weight in me,
As if by some instinct the wretch did know
His rider loved not speed being made from thee.
The bloody spur cannot provoke him on
That sometimes anger thrusts into his hide,
Which heavily he answers with a groan,
More sharp to me than spurring to his side;
For that same groan doth put this in my mind:
My grief lies onward and my joy behind.

William Shakespeare (1564–1616)

If Once You Have Slept on an Island

If once you have slept on an island
   You'll never be quite the same;
You may look as you looked the day before
   And go by the same old name,

You may bustle about in street and shop;
   You may sit at home and sew,
But you'll see blue water and wheeling gulls
   Wherever your feet may go.

You may chat with the neighbors of this and that
   And close to your fire keep,
But you'll hear ship whistle and lighthouse bell
   And tides beat through your sleep.

Oh, you won't know why, and you can't say how
   Such change upon you came,
But – once you have slept on an island
   You'll never be quite the same!

Rachel Field (1894–1942)

Up-Hill

Does the road wind up-hill all the way?
   Yes, to the very end.
Will the day's journey take the whole long day?
   From morn to night, my friend.

But is there for the night a resting-place?
   A roof for when the slow, dark hours begin,
May not the darkness hide it from my face?
   You cannot miss that inn.

Shall I meet other wayfarers at night?
   Those who have gone before.
Then must I knock, or call when just in sight?
   They will not keep you waiting at that door.

Shall I find comfort, travel-sore and weak?
   Of labour you shall find the sum.
Will there be beds for me and all who seek?
   Yea, beds for all who come.

Christina Rossetti (1830–1894)

Requiem

Under the wide and starry sky
  Dig the grave and let me lie:
Glad did I live and gladly die,
  And I laid me down with a will.

This be the verse you grave for me:
Here he lies where he long'd to be;
Home is the sailor, home from the sea,
And the hunter home from the hill.

Robert Louis Stevenson (1850–1894)

Terminus

It is time to be old,
To take in sail:
The god of bounds,
Who sets to seas a shore,
Came to me in his fatal rounds,
And said: 'No more!
No farther shoot
Thy broad ambitious branches, and thy root.
Fancy departs: no more invent,
Contract thy firmament
To compass of a tent.
There's not enough for this and that,
Make thy option which of two;
Economize the failing river,
Not the less revere the Giver,
Leave the many and hold the few.
Timely wise accept the terms,
Soften the fall with wary foot;
A little while
Still plan and smile,
And, fault of novel germs,
Mature the unfallen fruit.
Curse, if thou wilt, thy sires,
Bad husbands of their fires,
Who, when they gave thee breath,
Failed to bequeath
The needful sinew stark as once,
The Baresark marrow to thy bones,
But left a legacy of ebbing veins,

Inconstant heat and nerveless reins,
Amid the Muses, left thee deaf and dumb,
Amid the gladiators, halt and numb.'

As the bird trims her to the gale,
I trim myself to the storm of time,
I man the rudder, reef the sail,
Obey the voice at eve obeyed at prime:
'Lowly faithful, banish fear,
Right onward drive unharmed;
The port, well worth the cruise, is near,
And every wave is charmed.'

Ralph Waldo Emerson (1803–1882)

Love of Country

from The Lay of the Last Minstrel

Breathes there the man with soul so dead
Who never to himself hath said:
'This is my own, my native land'?
Whose heart hath ne'er within him burned
As home his footsteps he hath turned,
From wandering on a foreign strand?
If such there breathe, go mark him well;
For him no minstrel raptures swell;
High though his titles, proud his name,
Boundless his wealth as wish can claim;
Despite those titles, power and pelf,
Living, shall forfeit fair renown,
And, doubly dying, shall go down
To the vile dust from whence he sprung,
Unwept, unhonoured, and unsung.

Sir Walter Scott (1771–1832)

So, We'll Go No More a-Roving

So, we'll go no more a-roving
  So late into the night,
Though the heart be still as loving,
  And the moon be still as bright.

For the sword outwears its sheath,
  And the soul wears out the breast,
And the heart must pause to breathe,
  And love itself have rest.

Though the night was made for loving,
  And the day returns too soon,
Yet we'll go no more a-roving
  By the light of the moon.

George Gordon, Lord Byron (1788–1824)

Crossing the Bar

Sunset and evening star,
   And one clear call for me!
And may there be no moaning of the bar,
   When I put out to sea,

But such a tide as moving seems asleep,
   Too full for sound and foam,
When that which drew from out the boundless deep
   Turns again home.

Twilight and evening bell,
   And after that the dark!
And may there be no sadness of farewell,
   When I embark;

For tho' from out our bourne of Time and Place
   The flood may bear me far,
I hope to see my Pilot face to face
   When I have crost the bar.

Alfred, Lord Tennyson (1809–1892)

The Unexplorer

There was a road ran past our house
Too lovely to explore.
I asked my mother once – she said
That if you followed where it led
It brought you to the milk-man's door.
(That's why I have not traveled more.)

Edna St Vincent Millay (1892–1950)

Index of Poets

189

Index of Titles

Index of First Lines